MILITARY HOSPITAL NURSE

When Queen Alexandra's Nurse Sophie Allendale literally fell at the feet of Captain Robert Austin, M.D., aboard the ferry en route for a Military Hospital in West Germany, she soon realised that it would take more than a sprained ankle to get his attention. Robert had had enough of women to last him a lifetime, or had he?

MILITARY HOSPITAL NURSE

by

BARBARA NEWMAN

MILLS & BOON LIMITED
London · Sydney · Toronto

First published in Great Britain 1978 by Mills & Boon
Limited, 17-19 Foley Street, London, W1A 1DR

ISBN 0 263 72724 6

Set in 11 on 12pt Baskerville

*Made and Printed in Great Britain by
C. Nicholls & Company Ltd
The Philips Park Press, Manchester*

CHAPTER ONE

As the cross-channel ferry moved out into the stream on its way to the lock, Sophie Allendale turned from the rail, where she had been watching the dockers, to cross to the starboard side of the vessel. She decided to take a short cut through the lounge, but found a young man barring her path at the entrance. After an apology he stood aside to allow her to pass.

"Thank you."

She stepped forward as she spoke but caught her foot on the top of the sill, wrenching her ankle badly. She would have fallen had he not put out his hand to prevent her from doing so. Her first reaction was one of irritation at her own carelessness, then she turned to the stranger.

"Thank you again. You've saved me from a nasty fall."

"Perhaps in future you'll look where you're going." His voice was deep and scornful. This and his words made Sophie annoyed, although she knew that he was right, it *was* her own fault. She should have looked where she was going instead of gazing at this dishy stranger. Her hazel eyes grew dark with anger and in a voice she hoped matched his own, she told him,

"I'm sorry to have troubled you, but I *am* grateful for your help. However I'm perfectly all right now." Her usually pleasant voice was not only cold but decidedly remote.

During these moments of repartee she had been holding her foot off the ground and now, meaning to sweep away with pride and dignity, she put her full weight on it and was brought to a sharp halt by a severe stab of pain.

"Oh!" she muttered involuntarily, then flushed with annoyance that she had spoken aloud in front of this overbearing and rude young man.

"Here," he held out his hand and took her elbow. "Let me help you to a seat and I'll have a look at it for you." There was a gentler note in his voice now, and a faint condescension in his manner that infuriated her still more.

"There's no need, thanks. I can take care of myself."

"Perhaps, but I insist. I'm a doctor."

"And I'm a fully qualified nursing sister."

"All the more reason for you to show some common sense. If you're going to treat your patients in the same irresponsible manner, you won't be of much use to the Military Hospital where I presume you're bound."

That remark really made Sophie furious. The one thing she was proud of was her nursing record. She had been reassured on her abilities in that direction, and had she not won the gold medal for the best nurse of her year at St. Andrew's? That was no mean honour. She was about to retaliate, but what was the use of fighting an insensitive man such as this stranger?

Another and more sobering thought crossed her mind. He could be working at the military hospital in Radlau, in which case it would be stupid of her to alienate him now. Caution made her unusually wary. After all, so much depended on personal relationships among all the members of the staff, and their ability to work amicably with one another, particularly with the doctors. Swallowing her pride, she hobbled to a seat with his help.

6

The doctor's hands were gentle but firm as he mani-pulated the injured ankle, which was already showing signs of swelling.

"I don't think there's any irreparable damage. It's just a sprain. Have you a cabin?" he asked, looking directly at her, one eyebrow raised much higher than the other. His expression softened a little when he saw the softness of hers, and the shadow of pain in the hazel eyes gazing solemnly at him. There was a strength about the small oval face and the curve of the well-moulded lips that made him momentarily change his opinion of women, then his resolve hardened. Women were all alike, out to trap the first man who showed any sign of friendship. He admitted this girl was very attrac-tive with her red hair and the large eyes that looked straight at him, but *he* was not to be caught again by a pretty face. Suddenly he was aware that she was speaking.

"I beg your pardon?" Despite the words there was no apology in his voice, but there was a faint hesitation which almost amounted to a stammer. Immediately her trained mind noted the fact and her mood softened. Her voice was much kinder when she answered,

"I only said that I have a cabin."

"Then I should go there now, put a cold compress on your ankle and rest it as much as possible during the crossing." He helped her to stand up, but when he would have taken her arm to assist her she shrugged him off.

"I can manage." Sophie's voice still sounded cold, though she had not meant it to be. She deeply regretted her ungraciousness, but it was really his fault for being so rude! Perhaps abrupt would be a better word, she decided. With a gesture of defiance she swept back the curtain of hair that flamed like a tropical sunset with a hand that matched her finely-boned frame, then limped away.

Annoyed by her own lack of sophistication in dealing with the whole situation, she soaked some tissues in cold water for the compress and lay on her bunk, a small towel folded under her foot. She was grateful for the comfort of the treatment as she lay thinking about the young doctor.

"He may be good-looking, but he certainly knows it." That she was being a little unfair she admitted, but he was arrogant and probably ruthless as well, except perhaps where his patients were concerned. He certainly had been kind when he realised she had hurt her ankle.

"I wonder if he's in the army or just going to Europe for a holiday?" she asked herself. "Whatever it is, I hope he's not stationed at Radlau."

Her thoughts turned to St Andrew's, her training school, and to Doug. There was deep pain and hurt in her eyes now as she remembered her engagement to him and how happy she had been until his affair with Irene, the wife of his best friend. She tried to dismiss him from her mind but his image, and the memory of the night she had broken off her engagement to him, kept forcing their way back into it.

It was not just his having an affair with Irene, it was the lies he had told her. It had never occurred to her at the time to check if he really was on duty so often, though she had commented that he seemed to be doing more than his share of evening duties. He had made the excuse that he was helping out some of his colleagues and Sophie had accepted the explanation without question.

It was only when she began to notice the junior nurses on the ward talking together, and all too obviously changing the subject when she appeared, that she began to wonder what it was all about. Then came the evening when she mentioned to Alison, her best friend, that she would not be going out to dinner as she had hoped as Doug was on duty. Her friend's reaction was to look angry and to open her mouth as if to speak, and close it again. Sophie asked her outright, forcing the issue.

"Alison, there's something going on and I'm sure it concerns me. I've no idea what it is but you can tell me and put me out of this feeling of suspense."

Her friend hesitated for a few seconds, then Sophie added,

"Whatever it is I would much rather know. Have I done something awful?"

"No!" The word was explosive. "It's nothing like that." Again the hesitation before Alison continued, "Well, I suppose it will be better to hear it from me than from some other source, or to find out for yourself in some public place. It's Doug. He's having an affair with Irene Finlay, and I know he has been out with her when he told you he was on duty. He certainly isn't on duty tonight, that I do know."

"But with Irene!" exclaimed Sophie. "She's not only married to his best friend but she has two small children. I can't believe it."

"It's true. No one would worry if he took other women out, but Irene? She's such a naïve baby herself, so Doug is really to blame. She's probably flattered by someone as dishy as Doug taking her out. I'm sorry, love, I hate telling you all this, but it will be best in the long run. Perhaps you can stop it before Irene really gets hurt."

"Thank you for the truth. I know it couldn't have been easy for you, so thanks."

In front of Alison, Sophie had fought back the tears

9

and accepted the situation with as much dignity as she could muster, but once alone, she had given way to her grief. Being a straightforward and honest person herself, she had made up her mind immediately as to what she would do. It was not that she had stopped loving Doug, but she had lost her respect for him, an integral part of loving to her way of thinking. She telephoned him when she came off duty at five and, after some hesitation, he had agreed to meet her in the hospital grounds right away.

When they met she was still angry, but she had herself well under control. Her voice was cold and her manner withdrawn. Doug took one look at her and asked anxiously,

"What's the matter, darling? You look upset and you've lost your happy smile."

"I wanted to give this back to you." Sophie handed him her engagement ring in its white and silver box, but before she could explain he asked,

"But why? I don't understand."

"I think you do. You're wearing your guilty look. It's Irene, Irene Finlay, your best friend's wife. Not only have you taken advantage of Bill being away but you lied to me, not once, but many times. I thought you were a man of principle but obviously I was mistaken." There was a distinct tremor in her voice and her eyes felt hot with unshed tears. It had taken all her courage to do what she had done and now her bruised heart urged her to repudiate it all and run into the shelter of his arms, but pride helped her to keep her feelings on a tight leash.

"But, Sophie, you know it's you I love," protested Doug, "with Irene it's nothing more than a mild flirtation."

"That makes it worse. It isn't that I mind you taking

her out, but did you have to lie to me and tell me you were on duty? That's what hurts most of all."

Sophie had never seen him looking so lacking in self-confidence as he did at that moment, and she felt sorry for him until he started making excuses and blaming everyone but himself. "Besides," he ended, "you should never believe all that the hospital grapevine tells you. You should know how they exaggerate everything."

She shook her head. "Whatever you say I have made up my mind. Fortunately I never got around to cancelling my application to join the army – I heard only yesterday that I have been accepted. I've already seen Matron and handed in my notice, and I'm leaving on the fifteenth as I have three weeks' leave due to me, I report to the Royal Pavilion in Aldershot on the seventeenth."

"Then you really mean it's all over between us?"

"I do," she replied, at the same time feeling sorry for him. He looked so disconsolate that she had a sudden urge to console him but she held firm.

"Hullo!"

Sophie forced her thoughts away from Doug and St. Andrew's as she turned to see a girl of about her own age standing just inside the cabin. She was extremely pretty, with dark curly hair and a lovely figure enhanced by a well-cut, dark fawn trouser suit. She was obviously very sophisticated both in poise and manner.

"I'm Clare Barron, and I understand I'm to share this cabin with you."

"I'm Sophie Allendale. Welcome aboard!"

"Thanks, but what have you been doing to yourself? No broken bones, I hope."

"No, just a sprain. It would happen now, when I'm on my way to a new posting."

"Seen the ship's doctor?"

"Not the official one, but I have seen a doctor, a passenger I think he is." Then Sophie went on to explain how the accident had happened and about the young man.

"Tough luck, but maybe it won't turn out to be too bad, provided you take it easy. As you mentioned a posting I guess you're army?"

"Yes, I belong to the Queen Alexandra's Royal Army Nursing Corps. I'm on my way to the British military hospital in Radlau."

"So am I, that's luck meeting you. We'll be new QAs together. Incidentally where are you from?"

"Bollingham, just outside Hull."

"I'm from Devon, not far from Teignmouth, but I've been stationed at the military hospital in Colchester."

Sophie, looking at the green eyes and broad smile of the newcomer, felt a wave of gratitude for the meeting and knowledge that this girl was one she could be friendly with. Her own natural warmth and friendliness returned. The young doctor would not have recognised this Sophie as the same one he had met and helped such a short time ago.

"The doctor you saw, is he tall, dark and handsome with a slightly overbearing manner and the suggestion of a stammer?"

"It sounds exactly like him. Oh, he has a slight scar over the left eyebrow."

Clare nodded. "That's Robert, Robert Austin. He was at Aldershot where I did my training. His bark is much worse than his bite, but he used to terrify the student and pupil nurses even if they did think he was dishy. I'll say one thing for him. If anything went wrong on the ward he always did his best to back up the staff, unless of course it was something serious. Then he would wipe the floor with you himself, but he would never report you for a genuine mistake."

"Well, that's something in his favour," agreed Sophie.

"Rumour has it that his fiancée dished him for some guy who was stinking rich, though there's some mystery about the whole affair. Mind you, there were plenty of girls all too eager to console him but he ignored the lot. To my knowledge he hasn't bothered with a girl since. I would have been prepared to step in, but I had some-one rather terrific going for me at the time, so I wasn't interested."

"Well, he's not my type," responded Sophie.

"I must say I liked him better as he was," continued Clare. "He used to be such fun away from the hospital, but now he seems to prefer work to any kind of enjoy-ment. Once or twice I've seen him let his hair down at a party but he clams up again. He's a damned good medi-cal officer, the best MO we ever had on medical." With a sudden change of mood she announced, "I think I'll slip up on deck and see the last of dear, crummy old England. Goodness knows when I'll be seeing her again."

"I'll come too. My foot feels much easier now, thank goodness."

"Okay, I'll wait for you."

On deck it was very pleasant as some October even-ings can be, despite some low cloud and a hint of sea mist below them. Towards the west the sun, no longer discernible, turned the greyness into silver and gold edged with scarlet. Where the sky showed through it was like some exotic painting with the colours ranging from the palest of pink, through yellow and orange to flame, with a smudge of blue here and there, as though smea-

13

red by the brush of an artist intent on involving all the colours.

For some time the girls chatted about all aspects of army life and about different people they had met during their service. On Spurn Point the lighthouse stood clearly etched against the darkness of the land and the blue and grey of sea and sky. The pilot who had brought them out had almost reached the pier as Sophie turned to her new friend and explained,

"Spurn is a nature reserve. Dad and I often go there to birdwatch. It's only about twenty miles from our home. In the summer Mum comes too, and we take a picnic lunch with us and spend the whole day there. Unfortunately they've been having trouble with the tide during the recent high winds and were cut off from the mainland until they could repair the road. The scientists say that it actually becomes an island once about every two hundred and fifty years."

"I'm afraid I'm not a wild life fanatic, though I do sometimes enjoy the natural history programmes on telly. I have been doing a little birdwatching, feathered variety of course," Clare grinned, "on Dartmoor with a boy friend who's interested in that sort of thing. I hate to admit it, but I actually enjoyed it."

"I've always been interested, I suppose because my parents were. Even when I was a tiny bundle, Dad used to show me things and explain them to me." Sophie gazed at the fast-receding lighthouse and felt a wave of sadness as she thought of her parents. They would be missing her and would be anxiously awaiting her telephone call tomorrow evening telling them that she had arrived safely in Radlau. She felt a wave of gratitude, not only for the happy home life they had always provided, but for their great love and understanding when she parted from Doug.

By modern standards Sophie supposed she and her parents were old-fashioned but she would not change anything. She was happy with the way they were.

Clare broke into her thoughts. "Looks as though we're in for a calm crossing."

"Yes, thank goodness. Last time I crossed we had fog, but the sea was as calm as a mill pond. Have you ever been to Germany before?"

"No, but I had a lovely holiday in Vienna last year."

"Did you find it the City of Dreams it's supposed to be?"

"Not really. I think that went out with the last of the Strauss family, but it's interesting. You should go there some time."

"I'd like to," agreed Sophie. "Probably I'll make the effort while I'm in Germany, but first of all I want to make a success of my job."

"You will, but you must enjoy life too. Speaking of enjoyment, what about coming down to see if we can get some food? I'm ravenous! I stayed with my current boy friend and his mother just outside York. We had planned to have tea in Hull this afternoon, but we were held up on the way by a lorry that had turned over and shed its load of packages all over the road."

As they went in search of the dining saloon, Clare asked, "How did you enjoy your three weeks basic at the Royal Pavilion?"

Sophie laughed. "Once I got used to the army way of life with its traditions I enjoyed it, though it took me a little time to get used to the drill and especially the saluting. That embarrassed me at first, but when it was explained that it was not just saluting a senior officer but performing an act of courtesy to the Queen's Commission, I felt differently. I'm a keen Royalist. The course did me a power of good, gave me self-confidence, especially when I realised that I was a member of a damned good organisation that looked after their people better than most employers that I know of. Besides, I was quite proud of my uniform and of being *Lieutenant* Sophie Allendale, QARANC. Sounds impressive, doesn't it?'

"Then you're not army-trained?" enquired Clare.

"No. I did my training at St. Andrew's in London. Then I did a year as staff nurse, and six months at Catterick."

"Then you'll be senior to me, not that I'm rank-conscious. I have no intention of remaining in the force too long. I'm going to find myself a nice rich husband who'll keep me in a style to which I want to belong."

Sophie's first reaction was to think what a materially minded person this girl was, but there was a distinct glint of amusement in Clare's eyes and a smile on her lips as she spoke which disarmed her immediately and made her like her more.

"And you?" Clare asked.

"I shall make a career of the army. I'm off men in a big way."

"You'll get over that," Clare assured her. "You're not the hard career type, I can see that. Some nice guy will come along and make you change your mind. You're not tied up already, are you?"

"No. I was engaged, but I broke it off about six months ago."

"You'll get over that, too."

"I wonder?" Sophie asked herself. "It's six months and I still love him." Her thoughts winged their way over those months of pain and loneliness.

"Hi! We're here," Clare announced jubilantly.

When they had eaten a large and pleasant meal Sophie excused herself. "My foot has started to ache again so I think it will be best if I go to bed and rest it. It's going to be a long drive tomorrow. I'd hate not to be able to manage that. By the way, have you a car aboard?"

"No, I'm going by train. I had hoped to have a Volkswagen, but there was some trouble over delivery. However, Dad, who gave me half the necessary cash for my birthday, ordered one in Germany for me."

"In that case how about travelling with me?" asked Sophie. "I only have a mini but there's plenty of room."

"That's a super idea, and if your foot gives you any trouble I can take a turn at the wheel."

"Thanks! I must admit I was a little worried about doing the journey alone. I've never driven on the Continent. It's driving on the right hand side that worries me."

"There's nothing to it," said Clare. "It comes quite naturally after the first few miles."

"I suppose so. In any case, it will be nice having a companion. Well, I'll be off. Goodnight."

"'Night. Hope I don't disturb you when I come to bed, *if* I come. I have no intention of missing anything and there's usually dancing on board. You never know what gorgeous creature I might meet."

Sophie grinned at her companion. "Good luck, then. As for disturbing me, you won't do that. Once I get to sleep I'm not easy to wake. Have a good time, and I hope you'll meet your gorgeous man. If you're awake in the morning before me, give me a call, will you? I believe we get near Rotterdam around six. I'd hate to miss anything."

"As most people will be dashing up on deck around that time, I'll call you just before. Okay?" Clare laughed. "Besides, we mustn't be late for breakfast.

17

I've only Deutschmarks with me, so I can't buy anything until we cross the Dutch border and I can't stand being hungry, a chronic condition with me." She giggled. "I'm a real hog when it comes to food."

"Judging by your figure I wouldn't have thought so."

"No, thank goodness. Whatever I eat, it doesn't seem to affect my figure. I guess I'm one of the lucky ones."

As Sophie prepared for bed she thought of Clare and of the instant rapport between them. Although she found it quite easy to make friends, there was usually a short period of withdrawal on her part. Once she had overcome her initial shyness there was no problem. If only she could lose her over-sensitivity to anything or anyone new, or to a change in environment or atmosphere! This was a side to her character that she wished she could change, but so far she had not been very successful. As Alison had once told her,

"When I first met you I thought you were a cold, unfriendly sort of person. How wrong I was! You're the type who grows on people as they get to know you. Then they learn just what a warm, friendly little creature you really are."

"Alison, you're sweet," Sophie had answered happily.

"You've got to learn to relax, sweetie, especially where the boys are concerned. I've seen some of the students eyeing you and obviously wanting to chat you up, but somehow you always seem to discourage them."

Then Doug had come along and swept her off her feet, crashing through the barrier of her reserve, and Sophie had become much more self-assured. Now, as far as love was concerned, she was back at square one. If only she could maintain her self-assurance, she knew she would be all right; but already she felt some constraint in the company of men, and she knew she must overcome this trait as quickly as possible if she wanted a full and happy life. She *had* tried, but her bruised feelings had held her captive within the shell of her shyness except when she was on the wards. There with her patients she was a complete entity. If only she could maintain that same relationship with people she met socially!

A cold compress around her foot, covered by a waterproof head scarf, a dressing-gown to replace her dress, and Sophie was soon comfortably in bed and asleep within five minutes. She wakened a little after five. It took a few seconds for her to realise exactly where she was. Looking across at the other bunk, she was surprised to find that her new friend had not been to bed at all. Her dressing-gown and slippers were exactly where she had left them the night before. Sophie examined her injured foot and was delighted to find the swelling had completely disappeared. When she placed it on the ground she found that all the pain had gone too.

Washing and dressing quickly, she repacked the few things she had taken from her case, then, putting on her new camel-hair coat and a scarf on her head she went up on deck. She could hear a great deal of laughter from the lounge on her left, and presumed that Clare was with that party.

Above her the swish of wings and the raucous screech of the gulls made her look up. As she watched them she saw one swoop towards the deck a little to her left. Lowering her gaze to see who was feeding them she saw Dr. Austin holding out pieces of bread for them. More and more birds crowded around the area, each receiving the same treatment. Sophie was fascinated by the precision and speed with which the gulls took the bread in flight but when she saw the doctor look towards her she turned quickly away.

Leaning over the rails, she now watched the bow of the ship as it churned through the water, sending up great fountains of opalescent and jewel-laden spray. The sun, just peeping over the horizon, turned the green sea into one of turquoise and ultramarine. She was so absorbed in what she saw she jumped when a voice asked,

"How is your foot this morning?"

"Fine, thank you," she answered, determined to be more pleasant to the young doctor this time.

"You certainly look much fresher than you did last night. Slept well, I hope?"

"Yes, and you?" she asked, more out of politeness than real interest.

"Yes, though not long enough, but that's my own fault." He remained silent for a few seconds as he too gazed at the spray from the ship's bow. "I gather you're driving down to the BMH with Clare Barron. It's a good idea – she can take over if your foot gives you any trouble."

"Yes, and I'll be glad of her company," Sophie answered as she wondered how much they had talked about her, and just what had been said, and if he, like Clare, had stayed up all night. As though reading her thoughts he answered her unspoken question.

"I didn't get into my bunk until three, but I'll make up for it on the journey down. A friend is bringing my car to meet me at Rotterdam. I had some ignition trouble just before I left Radlau and couldn't get the repairs done in time. Fortunately I managed to get a seat on a families' plane from Münster."

"Are you at one of the Military Hospitals?"

"Yes, the same one as you, Radlau."

It was at that moment that the noisy party flowed out on to the deck, still chatting and laughing. Clare was among them, and seeing Sophie, joined her at the rails.

"Hi there," she called. "Gosh, am I tired? I intended going to bed soon after you, Sophie, but somehow the hours slipped by while we were talking and dancing. When I realised the time it was hardly worth bothering."

Sophie was about to excuse herself, but Clare stopped her. "Don't rush away, breakfast will be ready by now." She turned to the doctor. "Like to join us?"

"If Miss . . ."

"Allendale, Sophie Allendale."

"Sophie, meet Captain Robert Austin, MD, DS, MRCP, Royal Army Medical Corps." She grinned at them in turn before continuing, "Now that's taken care of in the best traditional manner let's go for some food."

It was precisely eight-fifteen when Sophie and Clare drove off the ship and got under way. Robert, driving a nearly new Mercedes, stopped alongside the blue Mini.

"If you'd like to follow me as far as the autobahn, I'll lead. By the way, this is Major Oliver Hepworth. Senior Paediatrician at the Military Hospital." He indicated a fairish man, a little older than himself, who was sitting beside him in the car. "You'll both be seeing a lot of him, no doubt."

Then without another word he slipped the clutch and raced off. A few yards ahead he slowed down to give Sophie time to catch up. From then on Robert drove at a steady pace, allowing the smaller car to keep up with him. Once on the autobahn he waved at them from the window, then, accelerating, he was soon out of sight.

Sophie felt a moment of panic but forced herself to be

calm. One thing she must not do was to allow Doug to occupy her thoughts. There was danger, both physical and mental, in that. From now on she must look forward, not back. She had seen too many tragedies during her five years at St. Andrew's to allow her own life to disintegrate because of a man.

"I must stay alert," she admonished herself. "I'm a fully qualified nurse, I'm twenty-four years old and supposed to be able to cope with any situation or emergency and not get into a flap. A fine sister I'll make if I carry on like this!"

Within half an hour the two girls were laughing and chatting like old friends, and any anxiety caused by driving on the right side of the autobahn no longer troubled Sophie. She turned to her companion.

"You know, I'm really looking forward to life in Germany, and having you along with me on this journey has made it a wonderful introduction. Here's hoping we'll both be very happy in Radlau."

"Them's my sentiments exactly." The girls grinned at each other and liked what they saw in each other's eyes.

CHAPTER TWO

THE journey was relatively uneventful. Sophie drove as far as a café just short of the German border, where they had lunch. Clare, who had no Dutch money with her, was quite sure that the proprietor would take German money if the amount Sophie had proved to be inadequate. They ordered a Dutch vegetable soup, followed by fried ham, sauté potatoes and peas, after having carefully worked out their bill from the menu charges.

"Can we afford coffee?" Clare asked, and giggled when they had finished the meal.

As she began to count out what Dutch money she had, Sophie asked, "How are you on washing up? I prefer to wash, hope you like drying."

"I don't like either but I suppose I'll just have to grin and bear it if it comes to the point. I can't see Matron bailing us out, can you?" she ended, giggling still more.

"Perhaps they'll take the rest in Deutschmarks," Sophie suggested. "I've plenty of those."

"Me too. Anyway, let's try," but when they asked they came up against a language problem. The man's English did not get any further than a few isolated words. Sophie's German vocabulary was getting quite extensive but did not include the words she needed at this moment. However, with the aid of sign language and an odd word thrown in they managed to get the bill. Sophie counted out her Dutch money and, placing it on the check, held up a ten Deutschmark note and asked, "*Kaffee, bitte?*" then pointing to the note said, "*Mit* this?"

"*Ya, ya,*" he answered, but when it was time to pay for the coffee he pushed the Deutschmarks back and added, "I give, please?"

"Thank you very much. That's most kind of you," Sophie answered. Then, gathering their things together, the girls returned to the car feeling that all was well with their world.

It was just after two when they arrived at the entrance to the hospital. After showing their NATO passes to the soldier on guard duty Clare, who had driven since the lunch break, asked the way to the QA Mess. There they were greeted by the Deputy Matron, who introduced herself to them as Major June Gladwin.

"I don't suppose you've had lunch yet?" she asked.

"Yes, thank you, ma'am. We had it in Holland."

"Good, but I'm sure you could do with some coffee. There's some in the anteroom. I'll check that it's still hot. It's that room over there," she indicated a large, comfortably furnished room on the right of the entrance. "I'm sure you'd both like to freshen up first. I'll get the mess sergeant to show you to your room. Don't be too long as the staff likes to get everything cleared by three."

"Yes, ma'am. Thank you."

The two newcomers were delighted to find that their rooms were on the same corridor and almost opposite each other. Each room was tastefully furnished. At one end there was a comfortable bed, a bedside and a dressing table with an upholstered stool, and an alcove with a washbasin and towel rails on which hung both bath and hand towels. Above the washbasin mirror was a strip light. There was also a table lamp by the bed.

At the other end, which served as a sitting room, there was a desk with yet another lamp, a hard-backed chair, an upholstered armchair, a bookcase and, much to Sophie's delight, central heating. The soft furnishings and carpet were an over all green in Sophie's room, in Clare's pink.

"The bathroom and lavatories are next door to each other around that next corner," the sergeant told them.

"Thank you."

"Will you find your own way down, or would you like me to come back in a little while?"

"We'll find our own way, thanks."

When they were ready Sophie and Clare went down together to the anteroom.

"The major seems quite a nice old stick, don't you think?" Clare asked. "And she has made us very welcome, thank goodness. I only hope Matron will be as nice."

The major was waiting for them and greeted them with the news, "I've contacted Matron and she would like to see you in her office in half an hour."

"Thank you, ma'am," the girls answered in unison.

"Should we change into uniform?" Sophie enquired, and the major smiled.

"No, this is just an informal meeting."

Sophie was called in first for an interview.

Lieutenant-Colonel Mary Rampling, Matron of the hospital, was a woman of about fifty, she judged. She wore an air of tranquillity about her that set Sophie's fears at rest almost immediately, replacing them with a quiet confidence in the future under this woman.

"Welcome to Radlau," she said. "I hope you'll be happy here."

"Thank you, ma'am, I'm sure I shall be." Sophie surprised herself when she realised she really meant it.

"Is this your first posting abroad?"

"Yes, ma'am."

"I hope you'll enjoy it, but remember, we're in a

25

country that was once our enemy and some of the resentment still remains among the local people, especially as they were very anti-Hitler and felt that their city should not have been bombed as heavily as it unfortunately was. It is only by personal contact that we can build up a good relationship, and by polite behaviour when we mix among them. Do you speak any German?"

"A little. I bought a grammar and have been teaching myself some ordinary words and phrases."

"Good!" Matron looked at some papers on her desk. "You'll be on Women's Medical with Lieutenant Joyce Carey who is, at the moment, on local leave until tomorrow. She will be your deputy. Sister Grant, from whom you are taking over, has been posted to the UK, but you'll have four days together. If you have any problems don't hesitate to come to me."

"Thank you, ma'am."

"Then off you go. I'll see you later in the Mess."

"Yes, ma'am."

Outside, Sophie whispered to Clare, "She's nice. You're to go in now. See you later."

It was just as she stepped on to the square leading to the Mess that she saw Robert Austin coming from the opposite direction. She was about to pass him, but he barred her way. In his white coat he looked quite different, and somehow more human and approachable.

"Hello, Sister. Just had your interview with the First Lady?"

"If you mean Matron, yes." Sophie heard the prickly note in her voice and softened it deliberately as she continued, "I like her very much, and I have full confidence in the future under her command."

"I wasn't criticising her. As a matter of fact she's very

26

popular, especially with the medical personnel. She's what you might call one of the 'old school', likes the old-fashioned standards and approach to nursing, and I'm inclined to agree with her. And she's not afraid of work. I've seen her roll up her sleeves and pitch in whenever there was a crisis of any sort."

"And yet she appears so dignified."

"Hard work doesn't make a human being any less dignified," he answered.

"I made no such suggestion. I was merely voicing my opinion of her after having met her." Again she heard the note of irritation in her voice and she strove to curb it.

"Don't be so quick in your implied criticisms. As for Colonel Rampling, unfortunately she'll be leaving us in a few months' time. She's being posted to the War House in London."

Angry at his rebuke, Sophie wanted to get away from him as quickly as possible. With an excuse that she had some unpacking and some letters to write, she hurried away. As she went she could feel his gaze directed at her back. What infuriated her most of all was the niggling feeling that despite his effect on her, she could not help admiring him, deep down, at the same time. He certainly was extremely attractive, and a type she had never met before. She hoped and prayed that they could reach some sort of a compromise and work amicably together.

The rest of the afternoon was spent in unpacking and arranging her bits and pieces around the room. When that was done she felt much more at home. A photograph of Doug lay face downwards on the bed where she had rejected it; she had set it in various places but had decided that, as she was embarking on a completely new life, it was time she forgot about all that had gone before. Doug was part of her past, the future was a challenge and she had never side-stepped a challenge if she could help it.

Picking up the photograph again, she took one long look at it then wrapped it in some tissue paper, put it in a suitcase and stowed it on the top shelf of the large built-in wardrobe. She knew it would be wiser to destroy it now but could not. When she was able to do that she would be really free. She lay on the bed for a few minutes to rest her foot which showed signs of swelling again, and immediately fell asleep. She was awakened by a knock on her door.

"Who is it?" she called.

"Clare. May I come in?"

"Please do. The door's not locked."

"Hi. You okay?" Clare asked anxiously. "Is the foot troubling you again?"

"Not really. I only meant to rest for a few minutes but I fell off. What's the time?"

"Time for tea. The major sent one of the sisters to tell us. I said I'd give you the good news."

Tea was a most pleasant affair, and gave the two girls added confidence in the future at the hospital. In addition to the deputy matron, a captain and two more lieutenants had joined them. After the introductions the captain asked,

"Which wards are you on?"

It was Clare who answered, "I'm on Gynae and Sophie's on Medical."

The captain turned to Sophie. "Then you'll be taking over from Amelia Grant. Her leave is overdue, as we've been rather short-staffed recently. I'm glad she can get away at last. She's been terribly busy and badly needs a rest. Your staff nurse, Joyce Carey, is most reliable and a nice girl. She's rather on the quiet side and is very self-contained, but then she should be. She's got the best of both worlds. She's married very happily and lives in married quarters. I'm sure you'll get on well with her."

"I'm sure I shall," agreed Sophie. "Is Medical very busy now?"

"Not at the moment. The 'flu hit everybody in the station so things got a bit hectic for Amelia. However, that bug appears to have done most of its deadly work and is fast disappearing. The labour ward is the hectic one now, but it so often is."

"Wouldn't it be nice if the back-room boys could come up with some drug that could regulate the exact time for all births?" Clare suggested. "It would make life easy for the doctors and midwives and let them have some normal sleeping hours." Clare grinned, then added, "Matron seems a nice sort of person."

"She is." It was the captain who answered. "She's a bit old-fashioned in some ways, but she does recognise and accepts that modern medicine has its place, and certainly advocates any new technique where it might be necessary. Incidentally, how do you feel about all this women's lib that gets so much publicity nowadays?"

"Fed up with it," Sophie answered without hesitation. "I'd go along with equal opportunities in pay, jobs, taking out mortgages and hire purchases. The rest I think is rubbish. Most of the married couples I know are happy and content to share everything, including washing up and even cooking. My father, except when he was too busy, helped mother. She has always maintained her own hobbies, which are painting and coin collecting, and has never been made to think of herself as anything but an equal partner in a very happy marriage."

"I think most of those that shout from the housetops are merely hoping to be interviewed by reporters and interviewers for radio and telly." Clare became serious as she continued, "As for me, I love being made a fuss of as the little woman and to be paid the courtesies and taken out. Besides I like my men to be virile and masterful. It makes life worth living. God help us if they become weak and browbeaten by overbearing wives!" Clare gasped for breath. "I do go on, don't I?"

It was Major Gladwin who broke up the party.

"Well, I know that if I had my time over again what I'd do. I'd certainly marry and have a family." Something in the deputy matron's voice made Sophie look more closely at her, and glimpse the pain in the steady grey eyes looking into space. Instinctively she knew that she, too, had suffered some unhappiness in the past.

"Gosh! Look at the time," the young lieutenant rose quickly and hurried away as she ended, "if I don't get back on duty I'll be in deep trouble. We have some admissions coming from one of the outlying battalions."

The others made their excuses, and soon Sophie and Clare found themselves alone.

"A nice crowd aren't they?" Sophie mused. Clare agreed.

What was left of the afternoon was spent by the two girls in roaming around the barracks and hospital precincts, and getting to know the layout of the whole camp. Sophie thought being with Clare was rather like having a series of guides. She had no inhibitions and asked anyone she saw, whatever their rank, what the various buildings were and where the different wards were situated. Sophie could not help smiling at the many looks of admiration cast in her direction and the many offers of personally conducted tours proffered to her new friend, all of which Clare declined with a smile and a cheery thank you. As they were returning to the Mess to have a bath and change before the evening meal a rather brash young man barred their way and, with blatant admiration in his eyes, gazed soulfully at them in turn.

"You must be the two new girls. I'm Dr. Martin Moore."

Sophie introduced herself. "I'm Sophie Allendale and this is my friend, Clare Barron."

"Pleased to meet you both, and welcome on behalf of the medical fraternity," he gave an elaborate bow. "Say! What about making up a foursome one night soon? There's a Dalmatian restaurant in the town where the food is first class." This time he looked imploringly at Sophie, who thought that despite his outrageous manner he was really quite a pleasant young man. "I'll show you the town as well," he added.

"That would be very nice, thank you," Sophie answered. "But it will have to wait until we've settled in and know what our duty times will be."

"That's okay, Oh ho! Here comes Mr. Loner himself. See you, girls. 'Bye for now!"

Sophie turned in the direction of Martin Moore's gaze and found herself gazing directly into Robert Austin's cold blue eyes. He wore a strange look, a look she could not define. Turning to Clare with a feeling of embarrassment she remarked,

"We'd better dash, or we'll be late for dinner. I'd hate to put up a black my first evening here."

Although Robert Austin passed them without speaking or acknowledging them, Sophie felt she had already done just that, but what exactly brought her to the conclusion she had no idea. It could be, she supposed, that he disapproved of anyone laughing and chatting with the young doctors in the hospital grounds. Whatever the reason, her dislike of the man was intensified, but she was determined not to dwell on the fact.

The following morning Sophie called for Clare.

"Sophie, you look super in your grey and scarlet. I thought the red cape might clash with your hair, but on the contrary, it complements it and really does something for you, especially with the white veil acting as a frame."

"Thanks," smiled Sophie, "you look pretty good yourself, but then you always do. But what about your medal?"

"It's here," Clare held up the silver medal with its red, white and blue ribbon then pinned it to the right side of her cape.

"There! I'd say we're a pretty good pair, even if I says it wot shouldn't," Clare grinned. "Come on. I'm looking forward to meeting the mums and their babies. I love Gynae."

"I'm quite happy with medical, though I think if I had a choice I'd go for paediatrics. I love kids."

Sister Grant, on Medical, was a little older than Sophie, a tall, willowy brunette with a quiet charm but a ferocious temper if any of her staff were found to neglect their patients. Like Sophie's, her patients always came first. She greeted her replacement cheerfully and with a warm welcome.

"I'm indeed glad to see you, Sister. I hope you'll like it on Med."

"I'm sure I shall," replied Sophie. "I understand you've been pretty busy with the, flu bug?"

"Yes, but it's eased a little. It was a pretty virulent bug, but so far we've only had one death from it. That was a very old lady, the mother of a member of staff. Anyway, I shall welcome a rest. Only three days to go, and then four glorious weeks of freedom before I take up my new appointment."

"Catterick, isn't it?"

"Yes, and I'm hoping to sit for my majority exam while I'm there."

Sophie nodded. "Well the best of luck. I was happy there. It's a very pleasant station."

Sister Grant looked at her watch. "We'd better go and take the report from Night Sister. She'll be anxious to get off duty."

After Sophie's introduction to Ruth Crabtree, the night sister, she told them it had been a quiet night and that most of the patients had slept well, "except for little Mrs. Armstrong in bed five. There's nothing tangible that I can see, but I've an uncomfortable feeling about her condition. She's not complaining about anything, but then she never does. Even now she assures me there's nothing wrong, but I'm still unhappy about her."

"We'll keep a close watch on her," Sister Grant assured her. "Have a good day; you're looking like I feel, overtired."

"I am too," answered Ruth, "and I'm going straight to my bed as soon as I've had breakfast. Going into town yesterday morning didn't help but I wanted to get some Christmas things to send to Jean Ratcliffe in Hong Kong. I've left it a bit late, but she'll understand."

When Ruth had gone, Sophie was introduced to the rest of the day staff, including her second in command, Joyce Carey, and Alice Marlow, the sergeant, all of whom Sister thought a great deal.

"They're solid, hard-working girls and most of them are extremely good nurses, even the pupil nurses. Young Rosemary can be a little troublesome at times, but she makes up for that at others. She's a temperamental, mixed-up sort of kid, though she's better than she used to be. Anyway, let's do a quick round for you to meet the patients before the medico arrives."

On the ward the stewardesses were busy setting up the bed tables for the bed patients, and the long centre table for those who could sit up for breakfast.

"It should be here any moment now," Sister Grant said.

Gazing along the length of the twenty-four bed ward Sophie's trained eye saw the tidiness of it taking shape and the general comfort afforded the patients. There were a few changes she thought she would like to make when she took over the responsibility, but there was no hurry. She wasn't going to be the new broom sweeping clean. She'd take it slowly and only after she had given the present system time to prove or disprove itself to her. To rush into change for change's sake would be irresponsible, and could easily provoke discord and even lose her staff's confidence in her.

"This is not a civilian hospital," she told herself, "this is another branch of the service and we're all members of the same family. Destroy that feeling of belonging and you destroy something unique and very precious." She was certainly looking forward to this new life. If only she could fill the void in her heart left there by Doug, she knew she could be very happy in this place.

The next half-hour was spent meeting the patients and taking a quick look through their case histories. She was completely engrossed with these when Sister Grant announced,

"Here comes Captain Austin. I'll introduce you to him."

Sophie stiffened. "We have already met, but do you want me to come with you on the round or shall I see to some of the treatments?"

"Come with us. You might just as well be in on it from the beginning. Tomorrow you can take over the

34

round yourself. I've quite a few loose ends to cope with before I hand over to you."

Sophie looked up to find herself gazing straight into Robert Austin's blue eyes. For a moment she imagined there was a hint of friendliness in them, but dismissed the idea as pure fantasy on her part.

"Good morning, Sister. How is the ankle?"

"Fine, thank you."

"You've already met?" Amelia Grant's voice sounded full of surprise, even though Sophie had already told her of their meeting.

"Yes, Miss Allendale had an accident on the ferry and I offered my services, but I'm not here to discuss my private life. Anything special to report?"

"No, Captain Austin – nothing definite that is, but Sister Crabtree told me this morning that she had 'a feeling' about Mrs. Armstrong and I never disregard Ruth's feelings."

Sophie waited for a sarcastic remark from Robert, but to her surprise he took the statement quite seriously.

"I'll have another look at her to make sure I've not missed anything, but don't hesitate to buzz me if you're at all worried. I'm on call, so I'll be in the Mess most of the time. I've quite a few letters to catch up with and some study to do."

"Yes, Captain."

The ward was light and airy and the central heating extremely efficient. As they began the round, all the old familiar smells washed over Sophie. She loved them and always found them both refreshing and, in a way, stimulating.

One thing she was assured about was Robert's work in the field of medicine. He was sure, quick in his movements without unnecessary haste, and had the perfect bedside manner. "Funny," Sophie thought, "he never shows any sign of his stammer when he's talking to them. It's only on social occasions that he does so." But what impressed her most of all was his infinite patience with the sick, even the difficult ones. She so far forgot her strangeness and joined in with the discussions, and even had the temerity to ask questions now and again.

At Mrs. Armstrong's bed she could not believe this was the same man she had met on the ferry. *This* man was filled with kindliness and compassion, and had that rare quality of being able to evoke a willing response from the sick woman who, until that moment, had been very quiet; too quiet, Sophie had decided earlier. Now she was smiling and answering all the questions the doctor asked of her. When they were back in Sister's office, Robert looked worried.

"There *is* something not quite right, but I can't find any cause for it. Her heart and lungs appear quite normal, and I presume her kidneys are working normally or it would be in the report. What about her urine?"

"Except for a few phosphates, all the tests are negative. There's certainly no albumen, and apart from her erratic temperature there are no obvious abnormalities."

"Good! Now what about that coffee you promised me? I could do with a cup."

"It'll be here at any moment." Joyce Carey joined them in Sister's office.

Sophie was about to wander into the ward when she heard Robert's voice, which held a challenging note, ask,

"Running away again, Lieutenant?"

Amelia Grant gave her an odd look, but said nothing.

"No," Sophie replied calmly, "I was just going to see some of the patients. I'd like to get to know them." To herself she added, "What a maddeningly discerning man he is!"

"Excuse me, ma'am." Rita, one of the ward stewardesses, held a coffee tray before her, waiting to pass.

"Sorry! I'll take it," Sophie offered, holding out her hands.

"Thank you, ma'am."

She would have much preferred to have her own coffee somewhere else, but she knew it would be ungracious to do so now. With her usual dignity she asked, "Shall I pour?"

"Yes, please."

Most of the conversation concerned the ward and the patients, then Robert asked,

"Have either of you seen the article about a breakthrough for the cure of leukaemia?"

"No, but it will be good news if it's true."

"It most certainly will be, but I haven't studied it yet. It's the result of some Australian doctor's research. It includes changing the blood of the patient for clean, uninfected blood." He remained silent, deep in thought for a few seconds, then continued, "I think I'll do some more blood tests on Mrs. Armstrong. It's only a shot in the dark, but it will mean I can eliminate one or two things it *might* be. I hate not being able to diagnose something."

"I'll see to it," Sophie volunteered, glad to get away from his presence which had the maddening effect of disturbing her in some obscure way. She sought out the sergeant.

"Captain Austin wants to take some blood samples from Mrs. Armstrong. Could you show me where the things are?"

"I'll do it, Sister. The ward is ready for Matron's round and most of the treatments are finished."

Sophie was about to refuse the offer but did not want to give the impression she was trying to throw her weight about, but neither did she want to go back to the office while Robert was there. She compromised.

"Let's do it together. We can get acquainted and I'll see where everything is at the same time."

When the tests were completed the report gave little information except for a low blood count.

"Well, we'll just have to keep a close watch on her," Robert told Sophie. "My guess is that it must be a virus infection of some kind. The temperature points to that, but with that kind of infection it's very difficult, in fact almost impossible, to isolate the actual type of virus. For the moment just treat her for the temperature and I'll write her up for something in case she doesn't sleep too well, and, of course, give her plenty of fluids and a light diet."

"Yes, Doctor."

At last Sister Grant had gone and Sophie was in charge with Joyce Carey as her deputy. Joyce was a homely person though a little brusque in her manner at times, but with a subtle and pleasant sense of humour. The ward appeared to be a happy one and Sophie was extremely pleased with her staff.

"It's a good team," she told herself, "if only the physician could have been anyone but Robert Austin it could have been perfect, but then nothing ever is perfect." As it was she had to keep a tight control over herself when he was doing his round, and whenever possible she deputised Joyce to do the round for her. The result was a cold courtesy on both sides. When one evening she mentioned something of her feelings to Clare, she was surprised to hear,

"That explains why he has been coming to Gynae for coffee the last few mornings. Apparently he always used to have it on medical. You must have made your feelings pretty obvious for him to switch. Anyway, what have you got against him? He's a good doctor. He's dishy, understanding and is quite well off. Apparently he comes from a wealthy family. His father is Robert Austin, the Harley Street surgeon; same name but with a handle. He received his K.B. in the last Queen's Birthday honours."

"It's his arrogance and patronising air that I object to so much," fumed Sophie. "I wondered why he hadn't tried walking on the water instead of taking the ferry."

"Hold on, Sophie! You're taking it a bit far. He's not as bad as that. Agreed, there's a certain arrogance about him, but it's only a veneer. Wait until you get to know him better. I know that somewhere along the line there was that girl, but exactly what happened I've no idea. Anyone who knew anything about the situation clammed up long ago. Anyway don't be too hasty with your judgments. Even a criminal deserves some consideration until he's *proved* guilty."

"Okay, if that will make you happy, but I know I'll never change my mind. He's a type I just don't like."

Clare shrugged. "Anyway, let's talk about something else. Oh, I forgot to tell you. John Illingworth, the gynae man, told me there's going to be a do in the RAMC Mess on Saturday night. Among other things it's a welcome party for us, you and me. He'll be contacting you personally, but he asked me to mention it so that you wouldn't make another date."

"What's the dress, uniform or mufti?"

"It's an informal do, so it will be mufti. I mustn't forget to put it in my diary, that is if I can find a space. This gay social life is getting too much for me. I must stay in." At this point Clare could no longer contain her mirth and her usual giggle made Sophie laugh too.

"I'm not used to having no fellas asking for dates," Clare added in a more serious mood, "but I guess that's good for my ego."

The Mess party started off rather badly but soon changed when Martin Moore arrived a little late with a girl on his arm. She was very young and very beautiful.

"This is Nan Buxted," he told Sophie and Clare. "Brigadier Buxted is brigade commander in Radlau, and these are Lieutenants Miss Sophie Allendale and Miss Clare Barron."

The music began at that moment and there was a rush among the younger officers to claim Nan as a partner. Martin turned to Sophie, but before he could say anything, she heard Robert's voice at her side. She was greatly surprised, as he hadn't been anywhere around a few minutes earlier. Sophie had looked.

"Let's dance," was all he said, and taking her hand walked towards the area set aside for dancing. Sophie was about to refuse, but her common sense and innate good manners made her change her mind.

Robert was an extremely good dancer and, though he was a great deal taller than her five feet three inches, he seemed just right for her. At first they danced in silence then Robert spoke,

"You look very attractive in that shade of blue."

Sophie looked down at the long blue skirt and matching blouse. She liked the outfit, but had not worn it since her break-up with Doug. "Thank you," was all she answered.

Her partner looked at her strangely and asked, "Personal associations?"

She nodded and quickly changed the subject. It was uncanny and most uncomfortable, the way this man seemed able to read her thoughts. He had done it several times on the ward, but she supposed it was this sixth sense that helped to make him such a good doctor.

"Have you really settled in now?" he asked.

"Yes, thanks. The only thing I'd like is to be busier. I hate not having something active to do all the time and, as I have such an efficient staff, I can't very well take over their routine jobs. Apart from Mrs. Armstrong, there's no one very ill to occupy one fully."

"Take advantage of that fact. Everything seems to go in cycles. It may be slack now, but tomorrow it could be hectic, as you must surely know."

"Yes, I do," she nodded. "Anyway I don't want to talk shop. It's one of the few things I don't like about nursing. So many nurses and doctors seem to have little conversation outside their work. I've always avoided it whenever I could when I'm off duty."

"I don't think you can really blame people for acting that way. They discuss their work because so much of their life is bound up with their jobs, but what would you like to talk about now?"

"Germany, and the people who live here. What are they like? Is their way of living very different from ours? That sort of thing. And the wildlife, is there anywhere within striking distance where one can see birds or animals?"

"Yes, there's a very good zoo in Münster." He sounded surprised. "It's said by some to be the second best in Europe. Personally, I haven't seen it yet. Perhaps we could explore it together?"

"That would be very nice. I'd like that." When Sophie said it she meant it, but regretted it immediately afterwards. Still, she did have to work closely with Robert Austin and it might even give them both a chance to understand each other a little better. As far as she was concerned he was a complete enigma. What puzzled her most was that few others seemed to see him quite as she did.

When the dance ended he thanked her courteously and left her. She did not see him again, and she concluded that he must have been called to an emergency. She was glad, because she felt much more able to relax when he was not around. Besides, Clare gave her no time to think about anything or anybody.

Clare, who was obviously a great success at the party and kept introducing her to more and more officers, told her,

"Martin Moore and Oliver Hepworth have invited us to join a party on Tuesday evening. They're going to that Dalmatian restaurant for dinner. It's in Münster but that's not that far to drive. You'll come won't you?"

"I'd love to! It will be nice to get away from the hospital and see something of the country. Robert Austin has invited me to go to the zoo with him some time."

"Has he indeed? But I thought you hated his guts."

"I don't hate him, I just don't like him," retorted Sophie. "There's quite a difference you know. Besides he is my ward's MO and speaks German well, and can help me with mine. I do so want to be able to talk to the locals if and when I have the opportunity."

"It's too much slog for me. I guess I'll get by with my own language. Anyway, I'm told quite a few Germans speak English."

"I think they do but I still want to understand theirs."

They were interrupted by Martin and Oliver. Martin's voice was light as he accused them of being too serious. "You should be full of laughter on a glorious night like this. Come on, Sophie! Let's show them how to really dance." He took her hand and pulled her on to the floor.

Like Robert he danced well, but unlike Robert he was inclined to show off by improvising all kinds of flamboyant steps which tended to embarrass her a little. At first she found him difficult to follow, but soon managed to match her movements to his. When the music stopped Martin was full of praise for her.

"I guess we make a pretty good partnership. I'd like to dance all the time with you but I'd better get my duty dances over first or I might find myself on the mat tomorrow." As he escorted her back to her chair he added, "I'm really looking forward to our date on Tuesday, and getting to know you better before the others get a chance to stake a claim. You're the most attractive young lady that's happened around here for a long time."

"Do you say that to all the new girls?"

"No, cross my heart and hope to die, as one of my small patients told me this morning. Seriously, I do mean it."

Sophie felt warm at his manner and responded with her usual natural shy charm. She was aware that he wasn't the type she would have chosen for a friend but he *was* attractive and no doubt his somewhat brash manner was nothing but a gay façade. Underneath there must be a sincere and thinking man or he would never have become a doctor and, she had been told, a good one despite his clowning and flirting. Yes, Martin could well be great fun to go around with. Just the right type to help her forget Doug, she decided philosophically.

When the party was over Martin insisted on driving her to her Mess, although it was but a few hundred yards away. When he stopped the car he turned to her and pulling her towards him, kissed her goodnight. His kiss was gentle and stirred her more than she cared to admit.

"Goodnight, Sophie love. I'm looking forward to Tuesday. We'll pick you and Clare up at around eight o'clock. Okay?"

"Okay."

CHAPTER THREE

SUNDAY, the day following the party, Sophie was off duty and slept later than she had intended. After a quick bath she chose to wear dark green trousers with a matching cardigan over a cream shirt blouse. It was much too late for breakfast but she had some coffee and biscuits in the anteroom.

"That's where you are! I've been searching all over for you." It was Clare, looking fresh and lovely in a brick-red trouser suit. "Oliver and Martin have invited us to go for a run and to have lunch at some *Gasthaus* a few kilometres away. Do say you'll come."

"It sounds super. Of course I'll come, but I suppose I should change."

"Why? You look gorgeous to me and that shade of green does something for you. Besides, they're waiting outside for us."

"All right, but I'll need a scarf and a warm coat. I'll bring my camera too. I want to get some pictures to send to Mum and Dad."

"Okay. I'll wait with the boys, but don't be too long."

Sophie only took five minutes, much to Martin's delight as he turned to Oliver.

"You see I was right. You owe me a pint of bitter."

"And what are you right about? Obviously it's something to do with me," Sophie asked, looking a little puzzled.

"Yes, I bet Oliver that you'd not keep us waiting for hours."

He laughed and the rest joined with him. This mood set the pattern for an exciting and happy day.

Although that part of Westphalia was very flat, Sophie was most interested in the houses with their neat gardens, clean façades and draped white curtains. Flowers and plants in nearly all the windows provided a gay, rebellious note against what to Sophie's mind was regimentation among all German houses.

"The lawns don't look up to much at this time of the year, but during the summer they're kept extraordinarily tidy," Oliver told them in his usual quiet manner. "In fact one lawn used to infuriate me very much because of its perfection, with never a weed daring to show its face. Then at the end of the summer one defector appeared. I've no idea what kind of a weed it was, but it made my day. Besides the weeds being *verboten* there are lots of other things one isn't allowed to do. You can only have a bonfire in your garden on certain days and at certain distances from the road, and you can't hang your washing out in the garden on Sundays. There are other regulations, but not having a house here I'm not sure what they are."

"Do they apply to British families?"

"Yes, we have to obey orders. By the way, have you taken your German driving test yet?"

"No, but I must get around to arranging it."

"See Hollingworth about that, he's Admin transport. He'll fix it up for you. There's nothing to it. The main thing is to know the German highway code. You'll be okay." Martin smiled at her.

"Any ideas about lunch?" Oliver asked.

"I think Bad Rothenfelde might be a good idea. The girls should see the thorn hedge. It's vast, and has been transformed from thorn to a rusty-looking iron thing by a continual flow of water over it. The chemical reaction is incredible. Crowds go to see it and to take the waters because of their reputed therapeutic powers."

"Do you believe in it?" asked Sophie.

"Let's say I'd have to see some cures before I'd compromise myself. Anyway, apart from the hedge it's really quite an attractive village, and there's a first class hostelry which serves very good food. I hope you girls are not too hungry as it's another half-hour's drive," Martin told them.

"What about you, Sophie, you've not had any breakfast?" Clare asked.

Before she could answer Martin pulled into a car park, saying as he did so, "I know where we can get some coffee and delicious cheesecakes, any variety you care to mention. They're really super, and will keep you going."

The snack was everything that Martin had promised. Both the strawberry and the orange cheesecake the girls ordered were delicious and they were tempted to have a second piece when Martin offered them some. Clare gave in, but Sophie held firm.

"No thanks. Much as I'd love another portion, I'd rather wait until lunch time, but I've made a mental note to have it with coffee whenever I go into town shopping."

"She's a girl after my own heart," Martin grinned at her. "I know just the place in Radlau where I'll take you. They have an almost inexhaustible supply of different flavours. I'll introduce you to them, but I reserve the right to take you whenever you want to go."

"That's a rash promise. I might keep you to it," Sophie said lightheartedly.

"That's precisely what I want." Although the words were lightly spoken, Sophie sensed the firm determination behind them. Martin really was serious, she thought, and the thought gave her a warm inward glow.

At Bad Rothenfelde they went direct to the restaurant, where they ate a huge lunch of veal steaks with spice and pepper sauce, followed by a sweet omelette.

From there they were shown the hedge. Sophie had never seen anything quite like it. It stood at least twenty-five to thirty feet high and looked like a wall of rusted iron filigree. Along the top of it water flowed from a perforated runnel, keeping the hedge continuously wet. At the base a narrow pool stretched its whole length, which Sophie judged to be at least sixty feet.

"Taste it," Martin suggested.

"No thanks! It doesn't look very hygienic to me."

"A few bugs won't hurt you. They'll help build up your resistance to infection."

"I've got all the resistance I need, thank you, but I will take some pictures." When Sophie had taken all the photographs she needed, Oliver asked Martin,

"Think we have enough time for a quick walk through those woods we went to before?"

"Not really, it'll be dark in a couple of hours. I suggest we go back to Münster, have a light supper there, and then on to Radlau and the Mess for a drink and a chat to finish off the day. What do you girls say to that programme?"

"Sounds super to me," they replied in unison.

Sophie enjoyed every moment of the day and she felt warm and happy when Martin walked with her across the compound to her Mess.

"It's been a wonderful day, Martin. I can't thank you enough."

"Just say you'll come again and that will be all the thanks I need."

"I'd love to." As she spoke she turned quite naturally

to him, anticipating the kiss he was about to give her. It was a gentle kiss that gave promise of a pleasant friendship. For the first time since her rejection of Doug she felt alive again, and the void within her seemed to contract a little. She was deeply grateful to Martin for that comfort.

"I must go," she told him, "I have to see to my uniform for the morning and I have a letter to write to my parents. I always write at the weekend."

"If you must, you must, though I wish it wasn't so, but there's Tuesday evening – I'm looking forward to that very much. It's still okay?" He looked faintly anxious as he gazed at her.

"Yes. I've arranged to be off duty at five so that I'll have plenty of time to get ready. And Martin, thanks for everything. It really has been a super day."

"Goodnight, love. I hope we'll have plenty more." Then he kissed her lightly and left her.

As she went to her room Sophie wondered about her relationship with him. He was a very attractive young man but he was a flirt, and he could be leading her towards yet another letdown if she wasn't careful. In her room she looked at herself in the mirror. There was certainly a new sparkle in her hazel eyes and a quirk to her well-moulded lips that had been missing lately. Well, even if he was not as serious as he would have her believe, the situation in which she found herself was indeed a pleasant one and was most certainly helping to restore her self-confidence. It was quite possible that in the end she might even fall in love again, and Martin, after all, was a very nice man indeed.

The following morning, as she hurried to the ward, a heavy frost like diamond chips mottled the grounds and buildings. High overhead two jets roared, leaving comet-like trails behind them in the rarified atmosphere. The branches of the trees, covered by shimmering frost-jewels, hung like the glorious crystal chandeliers of the old castles along the Rhine.

Underfoot the same crystals crackled as Sophie hurried across the quadrangle towards the medical block. There she found great activity and the nearest thing to chaos that could happen on such a well-run ward. Sister Crabtree looked quite harassed, an unusual state for the unflappable night sister.

"We've just had three admissions from the Garrison Depot, all ill with the 'flu. There's Mrs. Heseltyne, the Commanding Officer's wife, a sergeant's wife and a private's wife. I've put Mrs. Heseltyne next to Mrs. Furness in the corner. The others I've put next to patients with whom I think they'll have something in common. None of them warrant bringing in their husbands even though it is a rather virulent attack they're all suffering. However, that's a decision for Captain Austin."

Ruth Crabtree sighed. "I'm not sorry to see you. I'm thoroughly exhausted. It's been quite a night, what with one thing and another. Poor little Mrs. Armstrong hardly slept, despite hot drinks and sedatives. Her temperature was up again at ten, but it's dropped to just a degree above normal this morning. Incidentally, Robert Austin came to see her before he went to bed. He's quite convinced she has a virus infection, but there's so little treatment he can give her apart from treating her temperature and trying to build her up in order to fight the virus."

"He's sent a slide or two to London for investigation. Perhaps they can isolate it with their more sophisticated equipment," Sophie told her.

"I hope so. She's such a poppet, and never complains. Not like Mrs. Graham. That woman really takes more looking after than half a dozen normal patients, but thank goodness, the spot on her lung has cleared up so she'll be discharged soon, I hope. She has my poor little state enrolled nurse running round half the night attending to her. Anyway, that's all for now. I'm off to breakfast and bed. 'Bye!"

Sophie was desperately sorry for the new patients, as she was for anyone who was ill enough to need admission to hospital. To her every new patient was a challenge and her greatest pleasure was to see them responding to treatment and becoming healthy individuals once again. This was most exciting and satisfied some inner urge, and feeling that was an integral part of all good nurses.

Doing a quick round before the doctor arrived, she was amazed to find that Mrs. Heseltyne was a Hull girl and a friend of her mother's.

"I haven't seen your mother for nearly two years, as we were in Hong Kong before Jim was posted to Osnabrück," she told Sophie. "I was going home next week but I suppose this will put paid to that."

"I'm afraid it will, but I mustn't keep you talking. Rest now and when you're feeling better we'll have a good old chat."

When Robert came to Mrs. Heseltyne's bed during his round, he greeted her as an old friend.

"Nice to see you again, but not as a patient. You've had no recurrence of the old trouble, I gather?"

"No," she agreed, "I've been free of that, thank goodness. I hope it continues that way."

Later in the office, Robert explained. "Mrs. Heseltyne was here at the beginning of the year with acute pyelitis and was in a pretty bad way. She didn't respond to treatment for over a week. However, the treatment was changed and she forged ahead after that.

51

Incidentally, she wasn't my patient. I was on paedia-trics then, but I saw a lot of her when I was duty officer and I sometimes stood in for the regular MO who was a friend of mine and was studying for his Membership exam."

This long explanation, peppered with signs of his impediment, was the longest speech Sophie had heard from Robert. Usually his orders for treatment were delivered in short, erudite sentences. It was only with the patients that he carried on what appeared to be any uninhibited and lengthy conversations. Perhaps he had these expansive moods occasionally. Responding to it now, she told him,

"I have met Mrs. Heseltyne once or twice in Hull. She was a great friend of my mother's. They went to the same school in York, though my mother was senior to her."

"So you're a Yorkshire lass?" he enquired.

"I am, and I'm proud of it." There was a note of arrogance in her voice for which she was sorry when he replied,

"You have every reason to be. I served my two years' attachment to regimental duty with a battalion of a Yorkshire regiment, and was very happy with them."

On impulse Sophie asked, "Would you like some coffee? It's about ready, I think."

He hesitated before answering. "Thank you, yes." A few minutes later he surprised her still more by asking, "What is it like, living in Yorkshire? Although I was with the Yorkshire battalion, unfortunately most of our service was in Germany. Even when we were at home it was at Barnard Castle, and I was fully occupied with study for my exams. What I did see of it I decided would suit me if I could get into a group practice there. Do you agree?"

"It's the best county in England! My father is a doctor with a practice in Hull. Perhaps if you're there at any time you might like to call on him. He can tell you a lot more than I can, of course." The moment she had issued the invitation Sophie wished she hadn't. Robert might think she was trying to make a pass at him. That was the last thing she intended, but she was reassured when he answered.

"I might do just that as I'm not completely sure that I'll stay in the army when my time is up. I used to think I'd like to specialise, but I've washed that idea right out. I feel I'd like to have patients that I could really get to know as human beings, as well as people I'm treating. I'd like to be what the old family doctor used to be, a friend to them all. Someone in whom they can confide their troubles, as I'm sure half the psychiatric patients are so because of the lack of someone to whom they can talk and get rid of their inhibitions. I want something that does more for me than just provide me with my bread and butter." Suddenly his stammer became very much more pronounced than Sophie had heard before, "I'm sorry. Why should I bore you with my dreams and aspirations?"

There was no doubt in Sophie's mind about this young man's sincerity, and for a moment she had the strangest thought. *What a good husband he would make for some girl who could truly love him.* She was so surprised that she only half-heard his last sentence, but comparing him with her father she told him,

"My father thinks very much as you do. About thirty years ago he was offered an opportunity that would have led to a Consultancy and eventually a good practice in Harley Street. He talked it over with Mum, but she wisely told him she would go along with whatever decision he made. *He* had to do the work, so *he* must

53

make the final decision. As long as she could be with him, that was all she wanted. Well, he turned the London offer down and bought into the practice in Bollingham. I once asked them if they ever regretted that choice, and both were adamant that they had done the right thing. I agree with them, and I would have come to the same conclusion had I been faced with that situation."

For a few minutes there was silence between them, each wrapped in his or her own thoughts. Sophie kept wondering what had made her tell this man so much about her personal affairs. She did not like him particularly, though she did admire him. She shrugged the thoughts away and began gathering up the coffee things. It was just at that moment that Robert's "bleep" called him to the telephone.

"I'll be right over," she heard him say, then as he replaced the receiver he turned back to her. "I would like to meet your father one day."

"When you need the address I'll give it to you, or perhaps they may come over here for a holiday," answered Sophie. "There's nothing definite about their visit to Germany but it was mentioned, and I know my mother hopes to get Dad right away for a holiday. He works much too hard. You'll like them both, everyone does."

Robert opened his mouth to speak, closed it again and after a muttered, "Thanks," turned and left the office.

Sophie's feelings were decidedly mixed as she went in search of Sergeant Marlow, who was busy doing some late treatments. Anything at all complicated was done under Sophie's or Joyce Carey's supervision.

"The state enrolled trainees are to have a lecture by Major Haynes at three this afternoon. I've told everyone but Rosemary. If you see her before I do, will you tell her, please?"

"Yes, ma'am."

"How is she now? Do you think she's settling down at all?"

The Sergeant hesitated then answered, though somewhat reluctantly, "I think she's improving. I hope so, ma'am."

"So do I, Sergeant, and you, do you like being over here?"

"Yes, ma'am, very much, and ma'am, I'm enjoying working with you." Sergeant Marlow was obviously embarrassed and Sophie hastened to put her at her ease.

"Thank you. It's nice of you to say so, and I certainly like having you as a member of my staff."

"Sister." The voice was Martin's, and Sophie greeted him warmly as she joined him. He responded by whispering, "There's nothing I'd like better at this moment than to kiss those smiling lips. I'm sorely tempted."

"Don't you dare!"

"The patients would enjoy the sight."

"Perhaps they would, but I would *not*. Anyway, I'm sure you didn't come on to the ward to discuss kissing."

"No! I wanted to ask if you'd like to go to the zoo on Sunday. I know you're a wildlife fan. Oliver is asking Clare. It's her free weekend too."

"But how did you know it was mine?"

"I have a little bird that keeps me in the picture. I've also heard that a certain gentleman is taking his coffee with you now. You must have won him round."

"I don't know about your last statement, but he does have coffee with us, and why shouldn't he? It is his ward. But about the zoo, I've already promised to go with Robert. Sorry."

"When?" demanded Martin.

"We haven't made a definite date, but I will be going," she answered with conviction but wondered if he ever would get around to making a firm date. Perhaps she was being stupid by believing that he would ask her again.

"Mr. Loner is taking you out? Incredible!"

"And what's so incredible about that?"

"He's never taken a newcomer out during the whole year I've been here. Usually they're older or married and their husbands go along too. I can't believe that he's asked you."

Sophie felt hurt for a moment. Was she so unattractive that other people thought that she did not warrant an invitation to go out with them? If so, why did Martin bother if that was the way he felt about her? But she controlled her irritation as she answered,

"You must believe it. I'm going with him."

"I'm sorry, love," he apologised, "I guess I'm jealous. You're right, why shouldn't you accept his invitation, but I just don't like other people muscling in on my girl. See you Friday about seven, okay?"

"Okay."

By Friday Sophie had forgotten Martin's remarks and the evening at the Dalmatian was a most pleasant one. It had been fun reading the huge menu with the many strange dishes. Sophie and Clare both had veal done in their favourite peppery, tomato sauce, Martin had veal done with mushrooms and Oliver an onion and tomato omelette. Amid the laughter and the repartee tossed across the table between the four of them, Sophie realised that beneath Martin's banter there was a seriousness she had not previously suspected. At one period Robert's name came up and Martin surprised her by saying,

56

"He's not a bad bloke really, but he takes life much too seriously. Maybe our little redhead will draw him out a bit."

Clare, who knew about the invitation, answered, "I'm sure she will." Oliver looked bewildered and gazed from one to the other of his companions.

"What's going on?" he asked.

"Didn't you know? Robert Austin is taking Sophie to the zoo."

"Is he now? Well, maybe she'll help him to laugh a bit more and to enjoy life. He's such a damned good doctor I'd like to see him relaxing much more than he does."

"Maybe, but it's my girl he's taking out."

"I don't think you can claim exclusive rights yet, Martin."

Then Oliver looked at Clare and his whole expression softened, and Sophie realised that he was in love with her. She turned to Clare just in time to see the faint blush that suffused her cheeks. It was obvious that she was not indifferent to him and Sophie was glad, though she was surprised that the gay fun-loving Clare could settle to one man so quickly; but she could understand it. Hadn't she felt a sudden and complete involvement very soon after meeting Doug? She had had lots of invitations to go out with other boys but, for her, there had been only one man, Doug.

She shrugged the thought from her as she heard Oliver add, "Just let's say you've put in a claim."

"Anyway, the whole thing's a storm in a teacup. After all what's so important about a visit to the zoo? It's just a visit to the zoo. Let's change the subject," Sophie suggested, then asked, "If anyone wants more wine, let me have a go with the gadget. It's fascinating." She indicated the glass and wrought-iron wine pourer filled with a rich red wine. Oliver handed her Clare's glass.

The laughter that followed restored the fun of the evening, and from that moment the tension disappeared. Martin was his usual gay self as they drove back to barracks.

For the next few days life on Medical ran smoothly. Most of the patients were recovering and Sophie now felt she had been in Radlau and in charge of the ward much longer than she really had been. The only patients who caused her any worry were Mrs. Armstrong and Mrs. Heseltyne. Mrs. H, as the girls called her, had responded to the treatment for flu but had had a sudden rise of temperature followed by a recurrence of her old kidney complaint. She was immediately put on the necessary drugs and a special diet with increased fluids.

"Be careful to maintain the intake and output chart," Sophie warned her junior members of staff, but despite all the care that Robert and the nursing staff could give her, her condition deteriorated. Robert and his senior physician decided they should send for the Colonel, and he was at his wife's bedside within two days.

Sophie was on duty when he arrived. He looked tired and extremely worried, and Sophie's kindness responded to his need. She prepared a tray herself with coffee, some dainty sandwiches and some cakes that had been left over from the ward teas.

"That is most kind of you, Sister. Thank you very much. I must admit I didn't feel like lunch, so I'll appreciate this."

When Robert arrived a few minutes later he was worried about the Colonel. "I've never seen such a change in any man in so short a time. I only hope and

58

pray we can cure his wife. They are one of the most devoted married couples I ever had the pleasure of meeting. If anything should happen to her he would be devastated.''

Looking at the intentness on his face and the compassion in his eyes made Sophie aware of him in quite a new way. Just for an unguarded moment the curtain of his reserve was swept aside and she saw him as he really was, a vulnerable and ordinary human being who could be kind and compassionate. Now she knew there was also a great depth of sensitivity, but the change was purely momentary and the arrogance and coldness were back again. She stopped smiling, and with a curt "Excuse me" left him standing in the office.

Why did Robert Austin have the power to disturb her every time they met? she wondered. She had no idea of the answer, and it was not until some time later, when she met Martin, that she felt relaxed again. She greeted him warmly.

"It was worth coming to see you, just to see that smile. It looks as though you're really glad to see me.''

"I'm always glad," she replied and smiled again.

"What about a bite of supper in the village? There's quite a good pub there.''

"I'd love it, thanks.''

"What time are you off duty?" he enquired.

"Eight o'clock.''

"Then I'll pick you up around eight-thirty. Okay?''

"Okay.''

November passed and December came in with a roar of wind, rain and, later, snow. On the ward Sophie was as busy as ever. Mrs. Heseltyne had recovered both from the 'flu and the nephritis and the Colonel had returned to his battalion, a much happier man. Only Mrs.

Raynor, a diabetic, remained a worry. Her blood sugar had gone down, but despite insulin and careful dieting it remained at a certain level and refused to alter.

Sophie was well satisfied with the few changes she had made in the ward routine and her team was working well, except for young Rosemary, the SEN pupil nurse. The girl worked hard but she was always causing unrest among other members of the staff.

"She's one of those people who creates all kinds of upsets by innuendo, and is an awful scaremonger," Sophie told Clare one evening in the mess.

"Why don't you suggest a transfer to another ward? But not mine," she added quickly.

"I feel that's not quite fair," said Sophie. "I suppose we're lucky having only one troublesome nurse. No, that's not true. She does her work well enough but she never does it with a smile. Now little Katie Smithers, she's exactly the opposite. Whatever she's doing, or however tired she may be, if you ask her to do something she not only shows willing, but smiles at you as though you'd bestowed an honour on her. If she only had the necessary educational qualifications I'd persuade her to go for her State Registration and a commission. She's the one who's been taking care of Mrs. Armstrong, and it's thanks to Katie and Robert that she is actually recovering. Robert has never been able to find the cause of her trouble, but he's quite convinced it was a virus infection. Anyway, she'll soon be well enough to be discharged unless she should have a relapse and there's no reason why that should happen." Sophie looked at her watch. "Gosh, I'd no idea it was that late. Martin will be calling for me in twenty minutes. Thank goodness I've had my bath."

"Where are you off to tonight?"

"The Careys'. Joyce invited us last week when we

were at the Dalmatian having dinner. She and Clive were there with some friends from Osnabrück."

"Nice couple, but I must be off. I'm going with Oliver to see a police film. We're both suckers for that sort. 'Bye! Have a good time."

"I will, and enjoy yourself too."

As Sophie dressed she thought about Martin and for the first time fully realised how closely her friendship with him had developed. When she had first met him she had not been impressed by his brashness, and certainly never envisaged getting to the stage where their colleagues bracketed their names together for invitations. Well, did it really matter? One thing she was grateful to Martin for, and that was that thoughts of Doug had grown comparatively dim and it was only on very rare occasions that she thought of him. Even these thoughts were no longer poignant, but nostalgic for something she had thought was good but had found to be insubstantial and just a fragile thing broken by another pretty face.

"Never mind. Forget the past," she told her reflection as she lightly applied a little green eyeshadow, "goodness knows what the future holds, so enjoy the present." She knew she had given herself some good advice and was determined to act on it.

Her thoughts switched to Robert Austin, and she wondered what he was doing tonight. Was he taking a girl out or was he sitting in his room with his books? She deliberately dismissed him from her mind but the picture of him crouched over a book kept recurring and disturbed her pleasure. Why did even the thought of him have the power to disturb her almost as much as his physical presence did? Her thoughts were shattered by the shrill ringing of the telephone in the corridor just outside her door. She grabbed up her overcoat and bag, thinking it was Martin, but someone had already answered it. The voice called,

"Everyone to Block B! There's a fire and they're evacuating the patients as a precaution."

Pulling off her long skirt which could be an embarrassment to work in, Sophie pulled on a pair of trousers and grabbed up a cardigan and ran down the stairs and across the compound to Block B. Thank goodness that didn't involve Medical!

Men and women of all ranks and all branches of the service were already converging on the threatened area at the greatest possible speed. Strange to see senior sisters running, but for fire and haemorrhage it was permissible, and only then. Everyone was taking advantage of it now.

CHAPTER FOUR

OLIVER Hepworth, who was duty officer for the day, was organising the work force. He assigned Sophie to the children's ward, "Then help in Gynae when the other is empty."

Children's was on the ground floor and at the back of the building. Sophie lost no time in getting there. She was conscious of other people dashing past her and of doctors and orderlies manipulating various fire appliances, and from somewhere below she could hear the fire brigade men shouting orders and the clatter of their equipment, but above all, the constant hissing of steam as the water from their hoses made contact with the flames. The acrid smell of smoke and burning materials filtered into every corner of the building, irritating the fighters' eyes and filling their mouths with an unaccustomed bitterness. Some were coughing badly, but nothing deterred their work. Sophie would have given anything to know how bad the situation had become down below but this was not the time to worry about such things, she decided. Time enough when their job was done. The important thing now was to get all the patients to safety, then, if it was at all possible, to save as much of the equipment as they could.

When all the children were evacuated she was sent to the labour ward. Here the urgency was not so great as it was further away from the source of the fire, but it was also a little more complicated. The women here were in various degrees of labour. Two of the babies were not due for several days, but were now threatening to arrive at any moment. No doubt the shock and the emotional upheaval had contributed to this situation. Another two patients, brought in from outlying stations for precautionary reasons, were still walking around and insisted on helping with the evacuation.

Sophie doing everything that was asked of her went about it in a quiet and efficient manner. Once she was conscious of Robert with his hair dishevelled and smuts across his nose and cheeks, carrying a stretcher with a male SRN. Somehow his appearance, so unlike his usual immaculate self, made him seem much more endearing, and just for a moment she wondered what he looked like when he woke from sleep each morning. She dismissed the thought as ludicrous and concentrated on her work.

It was only when the last patient was evacuated from the block and temporarily housed in another ward that Sophie and her colleagues were able to relax. Apparently the fire had been caused by an explosion in the basement where all the apparatus for the central heating, hot water and lighting was situated. Someone mentioned a bomb, but that was discounted by a nearby fireman. Sophie looked at her watch and, to her horror, remembered her dinner appointment and that she had never even tried to get a message to her hostess.

"Have you seen Dr. Moore?" she asked of some nurses chatting in a corner.

"Yes, ma'am," one young girl answered, "I saw him going into the main office block a few minutes ago." Sophie thanked her and hurried across the large intervening parking space. There was a deep furrow across her forehead because of her worry. In the entrance hall Martin hailed her.

"Hullo, sweetie! I was just coming to find you."

"Oh, Martin, the Careys! I forgot all about them and they'll be wondering what has happened."

"It's okay. I rang them when the fire broke out and told them we'd be tied up, and then I phoned them again a minute ago as I'd promised. Most of their guests were from the hospital, so they've kept the meal back. They're very anxious that we go along, even now. As Clive told me, they didn't want to be eating roast duck and orange salad for the next week or so."

"Sounds delicious, and I'm suddenly ravenous, but how very kind of them. I'll have to wash and change as I certainly cannot go looking like this."

"Even like that you look good to me," declared Martin.

"You do my ego good. Thanks, I won't be long."

"Good girl. I'll wait for you outside your Mess. Off you go."

Sophie made it in nine minutes.

The Careys greeted them as though nothing had happened except they had whisky already poured for the fire fighters.

"Here!" Clive Carey held out a glass to Sophie. "Help yourself to soda."

Sophie, who rarely drank whisky, accepted it gratefully. Now that the crisis was over she realised just how tired and tense she was.

"I'll have to drown it a little, as I don't like the stuff."

"I know, but this time it's a purely medicinal tipple. Joyce is in the lounge. You know your way."

"Thanks."

The first person she saw was Robert. He was standing near the large bay window talking to a most attractive woman about the same age as herself. She looked like something out of the glossies with her long flowing pale-green dress. It was made of some soft, clinging material that not only enhanced her figure but revealed all the contours of her beautiful body. For a moment Sophie

65

felt envious of her, but dismissed the thought. Even if she had the perfection of line this woman had, she still would not like to flaunt it as brazenly as that. As for Robert, he was once more his usual immaculate self, but she had never seen him looking quite so animated or so happy. For a moment she felt what seemed to be jealousy, but immediately dismissed the idea as ludicrous.

"Hullo!" Sophie was delighted at the sound of her hostess' voice, "Glad to see you at last. I hear there's been some excitement." She turned to her husband who had just joined them. "We're talking about the fire."

"Was there much damage?" he asked.

"Nothing like as much as there could have been," Sophie told him. "Most of it was confined to the cellar and to the west corner of the building, mainly the offices. They had some slight damage but none of the wards were affected, thank goodness."

"And the patients?"

"Apart from the threat of one or two imminent births they're all fine. As far as the children are concerned, they appear to have enjoyed the whole excitement. I understand that most of the patients are going back to their wards in the morning."

"Was it necessary to evacuate them all once they knew they were getting everything under control?" Clive asked.

"Yes, because there was always the chance of another explosion. The powers-that-be had no way of knowing whether it was an accident or deliberate sabotage. Thank God it wasn't the latter, but one can never be sure these days, can one?"

"No, we certainly can't take any chances. Oh, how I wish the whole beastly problem could be resolved." Joyce looked at her watch. "Excuse me for a few minutes. The food is all ready. I just have to dish it up."

"Can I help?" Sophie asked.

"Not for the moment, thanks, Clive and I can manage. He's very good in the house. You try and relax."

At dinner Sophie found herself sitting between Martin and Clive's CO, but directly opposite her was Robert and his glamorous girl friend, whom he introduced to her as Mrs. Marie Webster from Osnabrück. Out of politeness she included them in the conversation from time to time. When she smiled at Robert he smiled back, but he never appeared to lose his expression of cool aloofness.

Sophie felt her discomfort rising. They were not on duty, so why didn't he relax? He was the most irritating and unpredictable man she had ever met and the only one who could make her self-conscious. This she strongly resented, but she was not going to allow him to spoil her evening. She had every intention of enjoying it and the comfort of a real home. Not that she was unhappy in the Mess – far from it. She was very satisfied with it in all its aspects, but, it was rather nice to get into a private house occasionally.

The rest of the evening was most pleasant despite Robert's mood. She liked Joyce and her husband and knew she could now claim them both as friends. Added to that she had found Joyce, not only a reliable deputy, but easy to work with as well. Sophie was just about to suggest to Martin that she would like to leave when she saw Robert turn towards his glamorous companion and walk with her towards their host and hostess, obviously to thank them and to say goodnight. Sophie, who had been about to do the same thing, now held back. She would make sure he and his companion were well away before she said her goodbyes.

When she got back to the Mess, Martin kissed her goodnight and for once she responded with ardour. When she left him she felt strangely happy, her earlier mood forgotten. As she lay in bed, her thoughts went back over the evening and her goodnight kisses with Martin. Was she falling in love with him? she wondered, but decided it was too early to be sure. She knew she felt a real affection for him and was grateful for his friendship and his great sense of fun. What was even more important was the fact that he certainly was helping her to forget all about Doug.

Doug! For a moment Sophie thought about him and knew that she still felt some love for him. The next moment she was asleep.

It was during his rounds one morning of the following week that Robert asked, "Are you free on Sunday?"

"Yes, I am," she responded, startled.

"Then what about that date at the zoo? I thought we could have lunch first and, after seeing the animals and birds, we might go and have a bite of supper somewhere if that suits you."

"It sounds a very nice programme. I'd love to come." Sophie surprised herself, not only at her immediate acceptance, but at the flutter of pleasure she felt at the anticipation of a day out with this man, the man she had thought she thoroughly disliked.

"Then I'll pick you up about eleven. I thought we'd better get it over before Christmas hits us. There's too much involvement around that time, not only with the social life but with the patients. It's a time, I think, when they need more understanding and more fuss made of them because it's a time for family. Don't you agree?"

"I do," she answered quickly but some of the pleasure

had gone from her. His words about "getting it over" had sounded as though it was going to be a chore for him. Obviously he suggested it now because of his earlier promise to take her there. She was about to tell him that he was under no obligation to take her anywhere merely to fulfil a promise but stopped herself in time. After all she had refused Martin's invitation. She would look foolish if she were to refuse now. She must go through with it and hope that it did not prove too difficult to maintain a pleasant and friendly manner.

She could not help thinking what an extraordinary and complex man Robert was. If only she could understand him life would be much more tolerable.

"Well, that's settled, so let's get on with the round," and there was the cold professional man once more. It was incredible how he could switch from one extreme to the other.

When they arrived at Mrs. Armstrong's bed he asked her, "How would you like to be home for Christmas?"

"Will that be possible?" A smile transformed the features of the thin, pale face of the patient.

"Yes, but with certain provisions. You must take it easy for at least a couple of weeks. No heavy housework, no rushing to the NAAFI and carrying great loads, and you'll have to keep on a light diet for a week or two."

"Thank you, Doctor." She turned to Sophie, "Sister, John is on guard duty this evening so he won't be coming to see me. Could someone telephone and leave a message for him? He'll be so excited to have the news. We were dreading Christmas with me still in hospital."

Sophie nodded. "Of course, but I'll come back and see you when the captain has finished his rounds."

"I hope her John isn't the helpless sort at home,"

69

Robert mused when they were away from her bed. "She'll need as much help as she can get for a while. If it wasn't for Christmas I'd keep her a bit longer, but I think she'll be happier at home. Anyway, she's a sensible woman."

"And her husband is a most helpful and considerate man, I understand, so I'm sure everything will be all right. Her son and daughter, both teenagers, are coming over for Christmas so they'll help."

"Good! That's how a real family should be, united at such a time," said Robert.

On Sunday morning Sophie was up early, but could not decide what to wear. Glancing from her window made the choice much easier. Everywhere was a carpet of virgin snow. A pale sun throwing light on it gave it a warm glow, and patterned the shadows in blues and browns. She was enthralled by the beauty of it all and decided to take a brisk walk before breakfast and her outing to the zoo. Pulling on her long boots, and wearing a matching skirt and pullover in a pretty shade of soft green, she added a long brown suede coat and a scarf over her hair. After a quick cup of tea she hurried out to enjoy the, as yet, untouched snow.

Overhead the branches of the trees were weighed down with snow crystals. Somewhere she could hear the twitter of birds. On the ground there were several species, including a blackbird scuffling for food near the roots of a tree where the snow had already been disturbed. Sophie felt her cheeks glowing with the cold as a strange feeling of exhilaration surged through her. It was good to be alive and, thinking of her day ahead with Robert, her heart gladdened.

During the last few days her understanding of him had grown as she had watched him at work. She had never met a doctor with such infinite patience and forbearance of his fellow men. Nothing was too much for him to do for them, even when he had had a bad night and little sleep. Even those who were most exasperating and complained of everything did not ruffle his manner. He certainly understands people and their problems, she had concluded. She was enjoying her walk in the snow, and several Germans she met on the way called a pleasant *Guten Morgen*. She smiled and returned their greeting. When she looked at her watch she was amazed at the time. She would have to hurry if she was to have any breakfast, and she felt decidedly hungry now.

Except for changing her topcoat for one made from the material that matched her skirt, she was more or less ready. She knew the outfit suited her well. Then she checked her make-up, which was a touch of green eye-shadow and some lipstick. But she spent far more time on her hair and it was shining like burnished copper by the time one of the Mess staff rang through to tell her that Robert was waiting for her downstairs.

He greeted her with a warm smile and hurried to open the car door for her. It was the same Mercedes that had piloted her to the *autobahn* at Rotterdam. Apart from a cheerful "Good morning" and a comment on the weather he remained silent until they were well away from the hospital and its immediate environs. Then, glancing quickly at her, he surprised her by saying,

"You're looking very nice, but then you always do, whether you're in mufti or uniform. Amazing how mufti changes your personality. On duty you're always so damned efficient and aloof. I feel I've got to be on my best medical behaviour."

"I like that! You're the one who is always aloof,"

she replied with a little irritation, "though not with the patients," she added hurriedly.

"I had no idea I gave anyone that impression. Interesting, I must watch myself tomorrow." He smiled and his whole expression changed and Sophie felt a sudden quickening of her heartbeat. Thinking about her reaction, she assured herself that it meant nothing, just a matter of chemistry reacting to his smile, but she had to admit that she *was* deeply attracted to him; the man she had believed the last one on earth who could do this to her. After driving for some time she caught a glimpse of a small church on the outskirts of Münster, which they were just entering.

"Isn't it attractive with those arches and that tall, slim spire?"

"Yes, but Münster has a lot to offer to those who really look. There are several buildings in the city that I like. I'll show them to you." As he spoke he turned right into a large park which appeared to be fairly full, but Robert soon found a space.

"Wrap yourself up well. I don't want you to get a chill." As he spoke he lifted the collar of her coat higher and ran his finger along the contour of her cheek. A little embarrassed at the reaction she had felt at the touch of his finger, she asked,

"Which way?"

"Through that exit and straight on."

Although she had been to Münster several times with Martin, it had always been at night. Now in the winter sunshine it looked a very different city. In the Prinzipalmarkt Sophie was delighted with the Rathaus. Its Gothic architecture rising from above its colonnaded front was most attractive. To add to its beauty there were lovely stained-glass windows, above which pilasters and stone facias led upwards to small Gothic spires.

"It's truly fascinating," Sophie murmured. Robert, watching her, with her head slightly to one side, a smile on her face, was intrigued by this animated and delighted girl. He had never seen her relaxed quite like this. Normally she made him feel uncomfortable with her air of disdain. If she remained in this mood, the day should prove both an interesting and pleasant inter-lude.

"This isn't the original," he explained. "It was destroyed in the raids in 1944, but it was rebuilt to the original design about ten years later. You must see the Hall of Peace while you're here. We'll have time for a quick look before lunch if we hurry."

"Good! I adore seeing historic places. That's why I love York. It's full of interest. My best subject at school was always history."

Sophie would have lingered in the great entrance hall with its paintings and carvings, but she followed Robert to the far end where he spoke in German to the man behind the information counter.

"The English translation about the Hall of Peace begins in about three minutes." Robert turned and led the way into a large chamber which she rightly surmised was the equivalent of our own Council Chambers. Its walls were of wood. Across the lower half of the wall were two rows of carvings which the recorded voice told them were the doors of the document cupboards. They depicted stories from the Bible and of animals and the legend of saints and comic tales. During the com-mentary Sophie stood there, lost to everything but the broadcast. There was so much she could not remember of what had been said and she decided she would return alone one day soon and make notes. Her parents would love to see and hear all about this fascinating place. She must arrange for them to visit her before too long. They would enjoy it all, but she had to find a place for them to stay first.

When the speaking tape ended Robert took her arm. "Did you know that Münster was York's twin city?"

"I did know, but I'd forgotten for the moment," she confessed.

"We'd best go and have some lunch if we want to see anything of the zoo. I think it closes at dusk, which doesn't give us too much time."

"I'm so looking forward to it. Thank you, Robert, for bringing me, and for showing me the Rathaus. It's fabulous."

"I'm glad you enjoyed it."

They had lunch at the same Dalmatian restaurant that Martin had taken her to on several occasions. The Herr Ober recognised her immediately and greeted her with a warm "*Guten Tag*" then lapsing into broken English added, "It is nice to see you again, Fräulein," he turned to Robert, "and you, Herr Doktor. Table for two?"

"Yes please, Franz."

When he had pushed in Sophie's chair, he handed them two huge menus then asked Robert, "You would like a drink, yes?"

"Yes, please. What would you like, Sophie?"

"A gin and tonic, please."

"Two, Franz."

Sophie, mellowed by her gin and the pleasure of the whole outing, was less inhibited than she usually was with Robert and began talking about the things she had seen and the things she hoped to see in the near future.

"Clare and I are hoping to drive to the Möhne Dam one day. I'm told it's very beautiful country around there."

74

"It is, but I should wait for the spring to see it at its best. It really is beautiful then. Speaking of your friend Clare, I'm told that she and Oliver are becoming very involved, though I must admit I'm surprised. Clare has always attracted men as a buddleia attracts butterflies, but I hardly recognise this new Clare. She has never been even remotely interested in just one man before, but I suppose these things do happen."

"Of course you've known her for a long time, haven't you?" asked Sophie.

"Yes, two or three years."

As soon as they had finished their mixed grill and salad, followed by *apfel strudel*, Robert suggested not waiting for coffee. "We can have some tea later if that's all right with you?"

"Fine, thanks."

The zoological gardens fascinated Sophie as much as the town hall had done. The place, with its lovely lawns and gardens, its lakes and thousands of well-housed, well-cared for animals really captivated her. She hurried from one enclosure to another, laughing and asking interminable questions. Despite the cold wind that had sprung up within the last half hour, many children, mostly German, were having snowball battles and laughing and playing. Sophie watched them for a time but was glad, when Robert suggested it, to get back to the covered way leading to and from all the sections of the zoo.

The light was beginning to fail when Robert suggested they find somewhere to have tea. "I think we're too late for the gardens, but we'll go back into Münster. I know of a small café that will be open. We can decide what we'll do after that."

It was during tea that Sophie suggested rather tentatively that she would love to walk round the city. Even after dark she knew it was well-lit, so there would be no difficulty.

"Then walk around the city you shall," said Robert. "Anyway some exercise won't harm either of us."

"After those gorgeous cakes and the huge lunch earlier I'm sure I need it."

"All part of the service, ma'am." There was a smile in his voice and in his eyes and Sophie, looking directly at him, felt again that flutter she had experienced earlier. For the first time she was acutely aware of him as a man. The realisation came as a great surprise to her.

Suddenly she found a new restraint taking over her thoughts. She tried to act naturally, but she was not very successful as it was not long before Robert too grew quiet, and though he was always courteous he wore his usual air of aloof detachment once again. Somehow all the fun of the day had faded. When he asked where she would like to have supper she answered almost against her own volition.

"I'm sorry, but would you mind if we went back to the hospital? I'm feeling tired now, but it's been a glorious day. I really have enjoyed it. Thank you very much indeed."

Although her thanks sounded, and were, sincere, she knew she was acting foolishly and quite out of character. Because of her, the day which really had been most pleasant was ending in this way.

"If that's how you feel we'll go back straight away," he replied.

The drive back was mostly a silent one and when Robert stopped outside the QA Mess he did not get out to open the car door as he usually did, but waited for her to open it herself.

Outside Sophie hesitated, then thanked him again.

"I'm glad you enjoyed it," he replied, and without another word put the car into gear and moved off. Sophie stood there for a few moments, then turned slowly and entered the Mess. She felt tired and deflated and full of regret at the way things had ended. She knew she was mainly the cause of it, but there was nothing she could do without giving away her feelings.

What was really worrying her was the thought of the ward. How would she get through the daily rounds with Robert and remain apparently uninterested in him? Well, it was no good worrying tonight. Best have supper, then a bath and go to bed early and read for a while. Thank goodness, she mused, that Clare is out with Oliver and won't be home until late.

She awakened tired and dispirited the following morning. Although she had slept well, it had been almost two o'clock before she had fallen asleep.

"You're very tired this morning," Clare whispered at the breakfast table. "What's up, a hangover or something?"

"Something!" Sophie said wryly.

"Did you have a good day?"

"Super, but we changed our minds and didn't go on to supper as we'd planned. But I enjoyed the rest of it, very much."

"Good!" Clare looked at her friend then repeated her earlier question. "Are you all right?"

"Fine, thanks."

"Well, I have some news, just for you. Oliver and I are in love and he's asked me to marry him, but we're not saying anything yet, so keep it under your hat. No one else knows."

"I won't whisper a word and, Clare, I'm very happy for you." Sophie was delighted. "Who'd have thought when we met on the ferry that this would happen for you? You haven't wasted much time."

"It's the very last thing I expected, certainly. Now if it had been you I'd have understood. You're a much more stable character. Incidentally, are you and Martin serious? I certainly get the impression that he is, but I'm not so sure about you."

"No. We're just good friends," Sophie giggled. "I believe that's the correct phrase. By the way isn't there a security exercise today?" she asked, in order to change the subject.

"Yes, but no time has been given. We'll just have to wait for the order then go to our places. That's all I know. It's an awful waste of good working time, but I do think the authorities are right to have them. You never know where the terrorists might strike. Much better to be ready when and if it does come our way."

"That fire we had the other day on B block proves how necessary training is. The whole thing ran like clockwork. I was very impressed. Anyway, I'd best be getting on. See you at lunch probably."

Reluctantly Sophie walked across to C block, feeling a little as she had done when she was at St. Andrew's and after she had broken with Doug. Only this time there were no obligations, no engagements to break. This was a one-sided affair, because Robert was not even aware of her as a woman. She was just the officer in charge of his ward and a newcomer to Germany who needed to be shown the sights. He had already made that clear. If only one of them could be transferred to another ward! That was about the only solution she could think of, but it wasn't likely to happen. Anyway, was she really falling in love with him? If she was, she must keep her feelings well under control.

Things turned out more easily than she had expected,

because over the weekend there had been several admissions, two of whom were very ill indeed; one a case of pneumonia, a corporal's wife, and a major's wife with a suspected gastric ulcer. These kept her fairly busy. Robert made it easy as he, too, had reverted to his usual professional manner. Even when Sophie thanked him for the outing, he was completely non-committal and accepted the thanks as though she had spoken about the condition of the weather.

Later that day Sophie was delighted when Joyce Carey asked if she was going anywhere on Christmas Eve.

"No," she said, and Joyce smiled.

"Good. We're having a party, will you come? There'll be quite a crowd, I hope."

"Thanks, I'd love that."

"It will be a buffet supper. Some of the wives are going carol singing. They'll finish up at our place, then stay on. You haven't been dragged in on that, I hope?"

"No, thank goodness! I'm quite tone deaf, so I'd be no use at all. I'd just put everyone off their notes. Are you singing?"

"Not me. Like you, I'm tone deaf."

The intervening days followed their usual routine. The new patients responded to their treatments, and two days before Christmas Mrs. Armstrong was allowed home. Her husband, who was a lance sergeant with a guards regiment stationed in Münster, came into Sophie's office and shyly thanked her for everything she and the staff had done, then presented her with the largest box of chocolates she had ever seen.

"My wife and I talked it over and we decided that chocolates would be the best thing. We hope you'll all like them."

"Thank you very much, and I'd like to thank you on

79

behalf of my staff. We're going to miss your wife. She has been a wonderful patient, and we're all very fond of her."

"I think she's pretty wonderful too." Embarrassed by his confession, he started running his cap round and round his fingers, then in desperation asked, "Are there any special things she should have apart from the medicines the doctor has given her?"

"No, but she must take it easy, and I'd advise a rest on the bed every afternoon."

"I'll see to that, and thanks to the commanding officer's wife, quite a few people have got together to help. Mrs. Ffoulkes, my company commander's wife, has offered to do the shopping for Anne when she goes to the NAAFI every week, and two of my mates' wives are coming in every day to help with anything they can. I've also managed to get a German woman to come in for a week or two to do the heavy cleaning. Of course I'll do all I can when I'm off duty."

"Well, good luck." Sophie turned. "Oh! Here's Captain Austin. I'm sure he'll want to say goodbye to your wife."

"Good morning, Sister, morning, Sergeant. Ready for off?"

"Yes, sir."

"Then good luck, and I hope you'll have a truly happy Christmas."

"Thank you, sir, and the same to you, Sister."

"I'm sure we will, and good luck," Sophie replied then added, "I'll see if your wife is ready."

When they had gone Robert, who seemed in a more relaxed mood than he'd been in since their outing, told her, "Mrs. Armstrong seems to think very highly of all the staff here, but she speaks particularly well of you."

"That's very kind of her. We've only done our duty,

but in her case it has been more than a duty. It's been a pleasure."

"Is Joyce Carey on duty this morning?" he asked.

"No. It's my afternoon off, so she has a long morning. She'll be on at one. Is there anything I can do?"

"No. I've had an invitation to her party on Christmas Eve, but I'm duty officer. I just wanted to tell her I'll slip over if and when I can. Usually it's not a busy time over the holidays. Anyone well enough is allowed to go home and those at home will stay put if they possibly can. I presume you and Martin have been invited to the Careys' party?"

"Yes I have, and I'm looking forward to it. Are you coming to our Mess party on the twenty-seventh?"

"Thank you, yes. By the way, we're having a ladies' night in our Mess early in the New Year. Will you come as my guest?"

Sophie blinked. "I'd be delighted. Thank you."

"Well, let's get going," he said briskly. "I'm due in theatre at eleven. One of my ex-patients is having a cholestystectomy and I promised I'd be there."

When he had gone Sophie felt decidedly light-hearted. Somehow the feeling of reserve between them seemed to have disappeared once again. It may well be only the spirit of Christmas entering into him, but long may it continue, she thought. She had no illusions or hope that he might think anything special about her. She had learned from Clare that morning that he often took members of staff, at different times, to the cinema or dinner somewhere. She was nothing more than another casual and part-duty guest.

CHAPTER FIVE

WHEN Sophie went to the Mess for lunch she felt more relaxed and happy than she had done for many months. Doug was no longer constantly in her thoughts, her friendship with Martin was better than ever, and her relationship with Robert was vastly improved. Despite the neutrality of the reserve between Robert and herself, she suddenly realised that his friendship had woven itself into the fabric of her life, creating a bond between them which a short time ago she would have said was impossible. She was fully aware that it was a fragile thing, but for the sake of her staff and her patients she was determined to handle it with great delicacy and not allow her quick temper to erupt and spoil it. Then into the peace of her content, a letter arrived and with it all the old doubts, the heartaches and the emotional gymnastics.

Because of an admission to the ward, Sophie was a little late getting to the Mess. As she passed the letter rack she glanced at her pigeonhole and found several letters there. The one on top was from her parents, an always welcome letter, but she decided to save it until after lunch. Hurrying to her room, she threw the letters on her bed and after a quick wash changed her uniform dress because she had spilt a little lotion on the skirt. It was the smallest of patches, but, always careful of her appearance, she was even more meticulous about her uniform. She bent down to pick up her cap which she had spread on the bed.

It was then that she saw the letter. There was no mistaking that writing. It stood out like an illuminated manuscript. She felt her heart contract and her pulse race. Her relaxed mood was shattered. For a moment she gazed at it, loth to pick it up; at last she stretched out her hand and lifted it with trembling fingers. Tearing the envelope in her eagerness to read it, she hesitated for a few seconds before actually doing so. It began with Christmas wishes then continued in a purely personal vein.

"I know now that you were right, darling, to break off our engagement though I admit I was very bitter at the time and said things I should never have done. I can only ask your forgiveness for that. I am not only sorry but terribly ashamed of the whole sordid interlude, though it was not all my fault. It is you, and only you, I love. There never will be anyone else. Can you forgive me and take me back? Just say the word and I'll bring the ring over to Germany personally. Please, Sophie, say that you will."

It was signed,

"Your ever loving, Doug."

There was a P.S.

"I got your address from your mother. I rang her on Thursday. Both your parents are well and are looking forward to seeing you before too long."

Sophie's emotions were so mixed that she could no longer think coherently. If this letter had come only a few weeks ago she knew she would not have hesitated, but now? Now that she could look at the whole situation more rationally she could see both sides of the picture. She could accept his repeated flirtations, and she doubted he would ever change as far as they were concerned, but it was the circumstances of that last episode with Alison that still rankled. Did he mean what she had just read or was it merely lip service? She was not sure, and doubted if she ever would be sure. She was shocked by the implications of that thought when she realised she did not quite believe him.

Questions came crowding in on her, questions which she felt she could not answer. Questions such as, had he broken it off or had Alison done so, either because her husband was due back home, or because she had realised just what she was getting into? Sophie knew Alison was a nice young thing. That was the word, young and unsophisticated. She was not even twenty years old, having completed only her first year before getting married and leaving St. Andrew's. Sophie could imagine her being caught by the glamour of a man such as Doug paying her court, but she could not imagine Alison getting in too deep. She was too much in love with her husband to do so, besides which, she was a very sensible girl.

Sophie's thoughts see-sawed from one extreme to the other. One moment she was eager to say she would forgive Doug, and the next she repudiated the idea. There was little doubt that she still loved him and knew that, if he had come in person, she would probably have capitulated; but he was not here. She was in a mental quandary but the one thought kept recurring, he had lost her respect and confidence. Without them love could be a very sterile thing. He had done this to her once. If she were to take him back, he could so easily repeat the performance.

Voices in the corridor brought her the realisation of the passing of time. She must put the problem from her for the present, so, pushing the letter back in its envelope, she hurriedly put on her cap and a trace of lipstick on her lips. Whatever happened, she was on duty in an hour's time and the messing sister would want to know why she was not at lunch.

It was half way through the meal that Clare asked, "You're very quiet. Is anything the matter?"

"No, not really." But despite her reassurance, Sophie noticed her friend glancing at her from time to time, a worried frown between her eyes. Sophie made an effort to snap out of her gloomy mood, and was glad to find that she was having some success.

"Don't forget our date tonight," were Clare's last words.

Sophie had completely forgotten that she and Martin and Clare and Oliver were going to the army cinema. She thought of calling it off, but decided it would be mean to do so and would spoil her friends' evening. Besides, it would be stupid of her to sit in her room brooding all the evening.

That afternoon the ward was quite busy and just before four Robert came to tell her that a diabetic patient was being admitted.

"She should be here in about half an hour." As he spoke he was looking directly at her, then continued, "Are you all right, Sophie?"

"Why do you ask?"

"Because you look sad, and there's an air of bewilderment in your eyes. Have you a problem that needs sorting out?"

No longer amazed by these moments of great perception by Robert, she smiled at him, affection showing in her clear hazel eyes. His own expression softened and he told her,

"You know, I never realised you had a dimple in your cheek when you smile like that until this moment. You've been keeping it a secret."

She could hardly suppress a laugh, and somehow her problem over what to do about Doug no longer appeared so overwhelming. If they had not been on the ward now she knew she would have told Robert about it and asked his advice. His view on most things was always so clear-cut and logical, but she was glad she had not blurted out her story. This was something she must solve herself. No one else could do it for her.

"It's nothing very important," she told him, "just a personal problem."

"Well, if you ever want a shoulder to cry on, mine's always available." He stretched out his hand and rubbed the side of her cheek very gently, a gesture that took her very much by surprise though she knew it was done out of pure kindliness and concern.

"Thank you. I'll remember that."

"You do, and now I must be off. I'm helping in the theatre this afternoon. Jonathan is reducing a depressed cranial fracture. A sergeant was involved in a road accident, and suffered head injuries among other things."

"Poor lad. Is he married?"

"Yes, and has four children. His wife and two of the older children were in the car with him, but they suffered only minor injuries, thank God."

"What's the prognosis?" enquired Sophie.

"Quite good. The X-ray shows no actual brain damage, but we'll know more after the op."

"Good luck!"

"Thanks."

The evening at the cinema was for Sophie a waste of time. She was so engrossed in thoughts of Doug that she hardly saw any of the film, although it was a musical, the kind she most enjoyed. Once Martin whispered to her,

"You're not with us, love. What's wrong?"

Conscious of her lapse of good manners she tried, and eventually succeeded, in thrusting Doug from her mind.

She would wait until tomorrow to write. Better to think more carefully about her reply, and not rush into something she might well regret. With a great effort she managed to concentrate on the present and the rest of the evening passed pleasantly for all of them.

The following day, at a Mess meeting, Sophie was appointed messing officer and so was responsible for the smooth running of the catering side of it. One of her first big responsibilities was the cocktail party on the Saturday after Christmas. With her usual eagerness to make a good job of all she undertook, she went immediately after the meeting to see the mess steward and the wines officer to consult with them and to assure them that they would have her support in anything they did provided it was for the good of the members. Being busy all that day, she had no time to ponder on her answer to Doug. It was only when she went to bed that she was able to give it her undivided attention. Thinking all round it, she at last decided it would be better in the long run to forget him and to write and tell him that, for her, there was no beginning again. She would write during her off duty the next day.

The letter she eventually posted was short and polite, but held out no future for them. Several times she was tempted to tear up the letter and write the few words she longed to do;

"I love you, Doug. Please let us be friends again," but she thrust the thought from her, and in case she should change her mind, posted it immediately. That, she thought, is the end of a dream and my first real love.

On Christmas Eve several of the QAs and RAMC officers, who were invited to Joyce Carey's for the party, arrived bearing gifts for their host and hostess. As a friend of her deputy, Sophie had bought a lovely hand-cut crystal fruit bowl at the NAAFI. It was a beautiful piece, and Joyce was overwhelmed by the generosity of the gift.

"Nonsense," Sophie told her when she mentioned that she had been too generous. "It's partly for Christmas, and also to say thank you for your friendship and your loyalty on the ward. You helped me to settle in very much more quickly than I might have done."

"It was a pleasure. I'll confess that I hated the thought of your taking over from Amelia Crabtree when we first met, but it only took you a very short time to win me over; I realised you were shy and then all was well, so it's thanks to you, too."

Sophie bent and kissed her friend. "Happy Christmas, Joyce, and let's hope we'll continue a happy relationship in work as well as socially."

"Amen to that." They were interrupted by Robert and Martin who, both being on duty until late, arrived together.

After the greetings the two men separated, Martin to help Sophie carry some canapés around among the guests, and Robert to chat with Major Irene Gladwin, the deputy matron. Somewhere Clive Carey turned on the record player. The record was of *Silent Night*. It was one of Sophie's favourite carols and sung as it was now in its original German, she thought it even more beautiful. She was engrossed in the enchantment of it when Robert interrupted her thoughts.

"You're looking much happier tonight than you were yesterday. Solved your problem, have you?"

"Yes, thank you." She was about to say more when she thought she heard English voices singing in tune to the record. She looked around, but none of the guests appeared to be singing.

"They're outside," Robert informed her, just as

Joyce opened the front door. There were five of the officers' wives, each carrying her own home-made candlelit lantern. Although their voices were not particularly strong, they were pleasant and their harmony was very good indeed. When the carol ended they all trooped in for a drink and something to eat. Sophie knew three of them, and was introduced to the remaining two. It was Clive who took their collection jar and passed it around the guests.

"It's all for a good cause, the Clive Carey Fund," he said with such a straight face that one or two of the guests took him seriously then joined in the laughter with the others. "No, folks, it's for the New Year Party Fund for the children of those serving in Ulster. Some of them aren't so well off that they can afford much in the way of presents, so we thought this would be a good idea." The response was excellent and those who had little or no money with them borrowed from friends.

"Are you staying now?" Joyce asked one of the singers.

"No. We have three places yet to visit, then we'll be back. We might do well at Thea's and Marie's, but I doubt if it's worth going to Tommy's. You know what a Scrooge he is. We might just strike it lucky and find him in an expansive mood. It's well worth a try, but what about some of the rest of you joining us? We can be back here in less than half an hour."

Martin, grabbing Sophie's arm, called, "Come on. It will be good for our souls and fun too." Several of the others followed suit, but it was Robert who was the more practical one and barred their way.

"For goodness' sake, Martin, let the girls put on their coats or jackets before they go out. How do you think the wards would fare if they all went down with pneumonia tomorrow?"

The girls broke away and dashed upstairs for their coats, and were soon on their way to the next army quarter, Sophie remonstrating that she couldn't sing a note.

"You can carry the collection box then," Martin suggested, a suggestion that was carried out and proved a great success. Even at Tommy's they received a generous donation, something quite unexpected, as one of the party remarked on their return.

"I could hardly believe it. Do you think he's had a visitation, just as the real Scrooge had?"

Back at the party everything was forgotten except the enjoyment of the moment and the delicious hot supper of savoury flans, a variety of vol-au-vents, hot sausages with several fondue sauces, hot mince pies and huge bowls of sherry trifle. A sparkling German hock was served and followed by liqueurs for those who liked them, and coffee. Bowls of mixed nuts, pretzel sticks and potato crisps were on every table. At midnight presents from the host and hostess were distributed to each guest; for the women there were lipsticks, perfume and various make-up accessories, and for the men, after-shave lotion, cigarettes or cigars.

"It must have cost them the earth," Clare whispered to Sophie, "but what a lovely thought."

"It's typical of Joyce. She's generous in everything, including her time and her kindness. She certainly made life very easy for me at the beginning on Medical. I'll be spoilt for Surgical when I go there. I understand that I'm taking over there some time after the New Year. Joyce is taking my job, Matron told me today, as Molly Underwood is going on leave, and as I spent my last year at St. Andrew's on Surgical, she thinks that I will be most suitable."

"Are you sorry to leave Medical?" asked Clare.

"Yes, I'm sorry, but I like surgical work, though I'm glad for Joyce's sake. She deserves her own ward."

"Martin will be pleased – he's changing to Surgical on Monday week," Clare reminded her.

"I won't be there for a month or two anyway." Momentarily Sophie thought of Doug. It was on Surgical at St. Andrew's that she had first got to know and to fall in love with him. She sighed, then fought down the rising nostalgia within her. That was all over now so it was no good dreaming about it. She must put him out of her mind and concentrate on her new friends and enjoy their company.

Earlier that day Robert had told her that a party of QAs and RAMC doctors were planning to go in a group to the army ski resort. She remembered it now, and as though her thoughts had been transmitted he appeared by her side right on cue.

"It's a good party, don't you think?" he asked.

"Super. The Careys are not only nice people but very generous. There must be well over twenty guests here and all have a gift."

"Changing the subject," Robert smiled down at her, "what about joining the skiing party I mentioned earlier? It's to be late in February, provided the snow is right. There have been some heavy falls in the mountains so, unless there's a sudden thaw, it should be good. If you come that will make ten of us including two infantry officers and their wives. Do you ski?"

"Yes, I learned in Scotland and managed to get some practice on a friend's farm on the Yorkshire Moors," Sophie continued, "I'm not perfect by any means but I can keep upright which is more than I could do a year ago. As for going with the party I'd love it."

"Good! We'll discuss it later as I must slip over to the ward. I promised to do a round before I went to bed.

Goodnight, Sophie. Happy Christmas," and bending his head Robert covered her lips with his.

Sophie was more moved by that kiss than by any she had had before. There was a magic in it that held her captive as she responded with warmth and happiness. For a moment nothing else mattered. Even when Robert left her the magic remained but she could not help feeling surprised by his action. It had been much more than just a kiss, it had held longing and something more, something she found difficult to define. Could he feel for her as she did for him? She hoped so.

Christmas day was the patients' day. It began with a short service held by the Chief Padre. When he had gone breakfasts were served, treatments and ward routines completed followed by a last minute checkup of the ward decorations which, this year, represented Christmas on the moon. Everything had been made by the staff, Robert and his junior physicians had created the space machine from plywood, cardboard and silver foil which stood in the centre of the ward. Discipline had been relaxed and there was a general air of enjoyment. There was only Robert's round to do and Sophie waited with happy anticipation. When he did arrive her spirits plunged alarmingly. He greeted her with a faint smile and a "happy Christmas" but it might have been any day and she anybody. The words, I did enjoy last night, froze on her lips as anger and disappointment fought for supremacy within her. She turned away to hide her feelings, her mind in a turmoil.

Obviously his kiss had meant nothing more than just a kiss and yet she had been so sure. She admitted that she was baffled by his behaviour. Either it had been just an impulse at the moment or, for some unknown reason he did not want any romantic involvement to develop between them. If only she knew what the barrier he had erected between him and the world was she could fight it, but what could she do against the unknown? When he had finished his round she asked him,

"Would you like a sherry? We've laid it on with some canapés for anyone visiting the ward. It's in my office."

"Thank you, yes," he answered politely then added, "I'll stay on and help with the dinners as usual."

"It's very kind of you, I'm sure," she answered without enthusiasm.

By the time they reached the office several members of staff, mainly from C block, had joined them. Even her disappointment in Robert's reaction could not keep her spirits down for long among the happy colleagues and the general air of festivity.

A full traditional dinner was served with all the trimmings and it was agreed by most of the patients that it "was a right good do" as a tiny Yorkshire woman put it.

"Our turn comes tomorrow," Sophie told them when they asked about the staff. "This is your day."

"And a happy one it's been, too," another patient announced.

By the time everyone was off duty that evening they were feeling tired but happy. Even Sophie had talked herself into a more optimistic mood for the future and decided that she would treat Robert as she had always done. Perhaps that way she would stand a better chance of breaking down that invisible barrier.

Sophie decided to telephone her parents after supper. When eventually there was a free line and she heard her mother's voice she relaxed.

"Thank you for the gorgeous cameo brooch and the books you and Dad sent me. They were just what I wanted. Thanks a million.

"How are you, Mum and how is Dad?"

"Fine, love, thank you. Your Dad's as busy as ever and you? I hope you're not working too hard?"

"No, I'm fine and enjoying the work." Sophie heard her mother call her father then he came on the line.

"Happy Christmas Dad and don't overwork."

"Happy Christmas and I'm not overworking. Keep happy, oh! your mother wants a quick word. Goodbye."

"I forgot to mention that we had a call from Doug for your address. I hope we did the right thing by giving it to him?"

"That's okay, Mum. I had a letter from him a couple of days ago," Sophie heard her mother's soft intake of breath. She smiled to herself as she answered the unasked question, "No it's not on again. Doug wanted it but I turned him down. It's no good starting that all over again."

"If you say so, dear, but I hope you've done the right thing."

"I'm sure I have, but I must go, Mum and what about you and Dad coming over for a break? Give it some thought and let me know. Perhaps when the weather is a little warmer. God bless."

In the days that followed Robert appeared to have relaxed a little and invited her out to dinner on two separate occasions. His manner had been friendly, no longer so aloof but not that of a lover. If anything it was almost brotherly. This Sophie resented just as she had always done because she wanted so much more from him. The only clue she had to his behaviour was one night at a small German restaurant where he had taken her for dinner. Sophie had mentioned his mother.

"My mother died when I was fifteen," he told her. "My father married again a year ago." There was a note of bitterness in his voice, and Sophie was forced to the conclusion that he did not approve of his step-mother.

She was careful never to mention his family again, but on the ward she found herself depending more and more on his ever-ready willingness to give advice or help with any of the daily problems. As a doctor he was everything he should be, dedicated, full of compassion and understanding for the weakness of his patients and a brilliant diagnostician. As a human being he appeared less complete but there were days when some warmth crept into his manner when they were in the office alone or on those occasions when he took her out but he had never repeated that Christmas kiss.

Away from the ward Sophie occasionally gave Doug a thought and wondered what his reaction had been to her letter. Knowing him, she could not help feeling that he would not give up as easily as she would like him to. She was sure she would hear from him again. Strange, she thought, I wanted to be everything to Doug once and now I can have that chance I no longer want it, but the man I want does not want me.

"Sitting here and feeling sorry for myself is not going to help anyone," she told her reflection in the wall mirror. "I'll go and see if Clare's free and have a chat, she might even come for a walk with me."

CHAPTER SIX

FOR the next few days every moment of Sophie's time was taken up by some aspects of duty. Apart from her ward work there was the Mess cocktail party on Saturday. As messing officer she was determined that the party would be a great success and the food as good as she could possibly make it.

"Fortunately the cook is first class, good enough even for a five-star hotel so there are no problems there," Jean Freeman, the wines member, told her.

"Yes, we are lucky, not only with Mrs. Hartz but with the Mess generally," said Sophie, and Jean observed,

"When I think what I'd have missed had I not joined the QAs I'm horrified. Apart from the comforts of a first-class hotel, I get paid for living abroad and am a member of what you might call one of the largest clubs in Britain."

"We sound like a couple of contented pussy cats," Sophie grinned at her colleague. "We'd better get on with the planning. I have a recipe for devilled shrimps that's out of this world. It's one of my mother's, and is a marvellous filling for vol-au-vents." She was silent for a few moments, then shaking the thought of Doug from her mind, returned to the planning, not only for the cocktail party but the menus for the meals for the week end.

The party was a great success and Matron made a point of thanking Sophie for "the planning that must have gone into the party. I really congratulate you."

"Thank you, ma'am. It's very kind of you to say so."

Robert, too, was profuse in his congratulations. "I haven't enjoyed anything as much as I have tonight. You and your team must have worked very hard indeed. A pity the ward has been so busy this week, but that doesn't appear to have disturbed you from your usual efficient self." He had been about to say more but one of the mess staff interrupted him with a message from the hospital.

"There's an emergency in Reception, Dr. Austin. It's an accident case."

"Thank you. Tell the sister on duty that I'll be across immediately." Then Robert turned to Sophie. "Sorry, but I'm duty officer. Good night, and thank you for a most pleasant evening."

"I'm sorry you have to leave, but I hope the patient isn't too badly hurt. Is it a man or woman?"

"Man, a private soldier from Münster. Goodnight."

Sophie was sorry to see him go because he had been in one of his expansive moods, and she always found him most interesting and pleasant at such times.

It was a few days later that Sophie announced to Clare, "When trouble comes it always seems to come in threes. I've had two, I wonder what the third will be?"

"Why, what's happened so far?"

"Young Rosemary, the pupil nurse I told you about, is causing trouble again with the other nurses on my ward. I've no idea as to exactly what it is she's doing, but I can feel the atmosphere every time I go on duty."

"How do you know it's Rosemary?" enquired Clare.

"Because I know my staff, and she's the only one to create that kind of temperature," Sophie sighed. "I'll have to try and sort it out this time before it affects the patients, and it will if it's allowed to go on."

"A good idea but what's the other one? You said two troubles?"

"That's personal, nothing to do with the ward, thank goodness."

"Sorry, but would you like to tell me about it, or is it *too* personal? The old cliché is true enough, love, a trouble shared is a trouble halved."

"Why not? Well you know I was engaged once and broke it off with a doctor at St. Andrew's? I heard from him just over a week ago, asking me to make it up again."

"And have you?"

Sophie shook her head. "No! I've turned him down, though I'm not sure if it was the right thing to do. I suppose, in a way, I'm still very fond of him, but I really believe that in the long run it's better to leave things as they are. Whether Doug accepts my decision is another question. He's a very persistent man and what he wants he usually gets, so he may not take my answer as final. I have an awful feeling I'd give way if we met face to face. The trouble is that whatever my feelings I could never trust him again."

"Poor love! Men can be awful problems can't they?" Clare did not wait for an answer but continued, "I used to suffer from it in a minor key, but where Oliver is concerned I'm the one who wants to hold on. Quite a change for me. Fortunately there's no problem, as I'm quite sure he means what he says and has no intention of ever wanting to end things either. In fact he wants us to get married quite soon. He's one of those men old-fashioned enough not to want an affair before marriage, and though I've been tempted once or twice, I'm damned glad I never allowed anyone to jump into my bed. Though there are times when I long to be possessed by Oliver I'm prepared to wait, though not for too long, I hope."

"I'm very happy for you," said Sophie. "I only wish my future was as clear cut as yours."

"Your time will come. What about Martin? Do you love him?"

"No, though I'm very, very fond of him, but in some ways he reminds me of Doug. They both like to flirt – though until Doug's last affair I never minded. Now I don't think I could feel deeply again about someone who has love affairs on the side even if they are only mere flirtations. I would never be sure again. Another thing they have in common is a love of fast cars and parties."

"It'll work itself out, love," Clare soothed. "In the meantime play the field and enjoy yourself. At least Martin is good fun. You know, a week or two ago I thought you might fall for Robert Austin, but I guess the chemistry is all wrong between you."

Sophie laughed. "No, I can't see Robert and me ever being very close. As you say, we just don't mix." She looked at the wall clock. "Gosh! Look at the time. If I don't get back on to the ward there'll be even more trouble."

Sophie's mind was troubled as she walked slowly and reluctantly towards the medical block. Chiding herself for her tardiness, she quickened her steps. The sooner she sorted things out the better it would be for the whole ward, and she *was* responsible for its smooth running. No good shirking duty because it was unpleasant.

Joyce was waiting for her in the office as it was her half day off and second lunch. There was a worried frown on her wide forehead as she quietly closed the door behind her senior.

"This must be the third disaster," Sophie told herself as she turned to her deputy.

"Anything wrong?"

"No, I'm just a little harassed as we're all behind with our work. You know I hate leaving things undone when I go off duty just as much as you do, but we've had two admissions right in the middle of lunch."

"Not to worry. I'll see to anything that needs doing."

"Thanks, Sophie. You're a real friend. Clive and I are dashing down to Osnabrück this afternoon to see some friends, so I did rather want to get off duty on time."

"Then off you go, but what is there outside the usual routine?"

"The after-lunch medicines, number seven and number ten's treatment and the new patient's antibiotics. I sent young Rosemary to the dispensary for them as soon as she came on duty – she should be back at any moment now. Here are the case histories of the new patients. Mrs. Docherty is in bed eight and Mrs. Ramsay in bed five. Bed eight is in for investigation for a duodenal ulcer. She isn't too bad, but Mrs. Ramsay seems to be suffering from a multiplicity of ailments. She's in with pneumonia, but she also has arthritis and apparently gets bad attacks of sinusitis. Her hands and knees are badly distorted but she suffers these in comparative silence, and I mean comparative. She's never stopped talking since her admission, though Mrs. Docherty says it's quite unlike her. She and her husband haven't been with the battalion very long, but Mrs. Ramsay is one of those aloof people who likes to be left alone."

"A pity."

"Yes, because I think it's not aloofness but extreme shyness. Now, having established communications with another person, she can't stop. That's one of the reasons I stayed with her longer than I need have. I'm sure it's done her a lot of good. The fact that her husband is on a course in England doesn't help."

"Well, never mind, we'll sort it out between us," Sophie said briskly. "Who's on duty besides Rosemary?"

"The new SEN and Helen. Alice Marlow has gone to second lunch, so she'll be back at two."

"Then off you go. Enjoy yourself, and give my love to Clive."

"Will do. Hope you don't have too hectic an afternoon."

"Thanks."

When Sophie had checked the medicine list to see that the new patient's treatment had been entered, she went down to see them.

"Mrs. Ramsay? I'm Sister Allendale. I'm in charge of this ward. How are you feeling?"

"Much more comfortable now that I've settled down, thanks."

"Good! Nurse has gone for your medicine, so as soon as she returns I'll send it down to you. Twenty-four hours' treatment and you should be feeling much better." Sophie stood watching the patient's breathing. Obviously she had a great deal of pain, judging by the shallowness of her breathing and the sudden pauses between the breaths. Sophie remembered once when she herself had had pleurisy, how much pain deep breathing could cause. Now, as she gazed at the flushed cheeks and the lines of suffering etched around the woman's eyes and mouth, a deep compassion surged through her. Unfortunately there was nothing more that could be done at the moment except rest and sleep. They were both wonderful healers. There were questions Sophie wanted to ask for herself, but too much talking at this stage could only exhaust her patient and retard her recovery. She would see that she made up for it when she was better. Perhaps she could encourage Mrs. Docherty, since she belonged to the same unit, to help in bringing Mrs. Ramsay out of her shyness.

"Poor thing!" she told herself as she moved towards the other patient's bed. "She has far too much to contend with. Those of us who have good health should thank God daily for it."

Mrs. Docherty, unlike the pneumonia case, was a cheerful and large woman who laughed at everything and made the bed and her large stomach shake violently. She was obviously a kindly woman, who appeared to take the threat of a duodenal ulcer very calmly.

"Well, the investigations won't take long and if you'd like to get up after the doctor has been, I'm sure that will be all right provided you take things easy," Sophie told her. "Dr. Austin will be coming as soon as he gets back from lunch."

"Thanks, Sister."

Rosemary came towards Sophie as she moved away.

"Here are the medicines, ma'am. Do you want me to give them out?"

"No, Helen can do that, but be sure and tell her to check the medicine list first. I want you to do number ten's treatment. You've done it several times, so know all about it."

"Yes, ma'am."

"When you've done that you can get on with your usual work."

Sophie continued to do a quick round of the ward to ensure that all was well. She had always done this because she felt it was part of her responsibility as the sister-in-charge to be available for any complaints by her patients. She had just finished when she saw Robert disappearing into her office. She joined him there. He was reading the case histories of the two new patients which she had left on the desk for him.

"Hullo, Sophie. How are the admissions? Have they started their treatment yet?"

"Yes, the medicines have just come back from the dispensary. The ulcer patient doesn't seem too bad, but Mrs. Ramsay looks a little distressed because of her breathing. The pain is quite severe, I'm sure."

"Well, let's see them. I'll do the ulcer first."

It was when Robert had just about finished examining Mrs. Ramsay that another patient two beds away started calling for him in a loud, coarse voice. Helen, her hand on the medicine trolley, was standing beside her and looking thoroughly frightened. Her brown eyes, usually bright, happy-looking eyes, were wide with fear.

"This is it. The third disaster," Sophie told herself.

Robert, who had hurried to her side in order to calm her, asked quietly, "Please keep your voice down, Mrs. Rosenthal. There are other patients who need perfect quietness. Now what's the matter?"

"Nurse Raynes is trying to poison me. Gave me the wrong medicine, and it was the most awful stuff."

Sophie turned to the young nurse. She could not help feeling sorry for her when she saw the pale face and the trembling lips.

"Whose medicine did you give to Mrs. Rosenthal?" she asked, hardly daring to breathe as she awaited the answer.

"The new patient's, Mrs. Ramsay's."

"Not the tablets, I hope?"

"No, Sister, the medicine."

"Thank God," Sophie whispered, then louder,

"Thank you, nurse. Now go to the duty room and wait for me there."

"Yes, ma'am," the girl answered, and fled.

It was a very relieved Sophie who turned now to Robert, who in the meantime had managed to calm Mrs. Rosenthal down quite considerably. The woman's normally hard mouth was almost smiling now, and she was obviously delighted with the whole situation and proud of her dramatization of it and the attention she had attracted to herself.

"So, if you'll excuse me," he was saying, "I must go and see my patients on another ward. I'm sure Sister will ensure it never happens again."

"That's as may be, but it *was* the wrong medicine, and could have poisoned me," she snapped at Sophie, who was about to follow Robert.

"First of all, Nurse had no intention of harming you in any way, and the medicine she gave you was nothing more than a mild cough mixture which won't do you any damage whatsoever. If anything it might have the opposite effect, and stop that nasty little cough you have from time to time."

"That's what you say, but it *was* the wrong medicine."

"I know, and I'm very sorry. I'll see Nurse and reprimand her, but I hope that will be the end of it all. There's been no real harm done, and I'm sure Nurse will not make the same mistake again."

"I shall tell the Colonel when he comes to the ward."

"That is your privilege, Mrs. Rosenthal. Now I must see to my duties." Sophie made a dignified withdrawal and hurried to join Robert in the office. His face was full of anger as he spoke.

"I hold you responsible for the mistake. If your girls

were properly trained they would be sure to check all medicines before giving them to the patients, or if they are incapable of doing that, they have no right to be here."

Sophie stiffened. "Yes, *sir*, and as far as the responsibility is concerned I accept that without question, but I do reserve the right to deal with it personally. If more is needed I can send Nurse to Matron, but I am quite sure that won't be necessary. Helen is a good nurse and a very reliable one. We are not all so infallible that we don't make an occasional mistake. However, I apologise that you were bothered to such a degree, and I assure you that it won't happen again." Sophie's voice was cold with anger, but she was full of dignity. She had no intention of letting him see how disturbed she was by the whole incident. She admitted to herself that it *could* have had disastrous results, but in this case it had not been so, but she was not prepared to admit anything more to this over-bumptious, arrogant man.

"Well, the question of who is to accept the ultimate responsibility is irrelevant. What is important is that it *could* have had very serious consequences and done irreparable harm. What exactly was she given?"

"An expectorant," snapped Sophie.

"That's something, anyway."

"Yes, *sir*."

Robert looked at Sophie's unsmiling face and angry eyes, and with a curt, "If you need me I'll be in Men's Medical for the next half-hour," and without giving her time to answer, he turned and disappeared.

The sergeant, who had been to second lunch, came into the office immediately after Robert's disappearance. One look at her superior's face told her all there was to know.

"Anything wrong, ma'am?" she asked.

"Yes. Young Helen has given Mrs. Rosenthal the wrong medicine."

"Oh no!" The sergeant hesitated before continuing, "I feel in a way to blame. I should have given out the routine medicines before I went to lunch, but Sister said it would be all right to do them when I got back."

"Of course that would have been all right, but if anything goes wrong it's my ultimate responsibility, not yours."

"Yes, ma'am, but Helen isn't herself or this would never have happened, I'm quite sure of that. She's a damned good nurse." Sophie was surprised at the anger in the sergeant's voice. Normally she was a softly-spoken, placid girl with an extremely pleasant manner.

"Do you know why she was upset?" she asked.

"Yes, ma'am." the Sergeant hesitated then, making up her mind, began to speak, the words almost tripping over each other. "Rosemary was teasing her about her new boy friend. He's a private soldier and an awfully nice lad. Apparently he took Rosemary to one or two dances in the barracks before he met Helen. Since then he and Helen have been going steady. I think it's nothing but jealousy on Rosemary's part, because there was never anything serious between her and the soldier."

"That little madam again! I had a feeling this morning there was something wrong and that she was at the bottom of it. She certainly causes more trouble than the rest of the team put together. I've been meaning to have a talk with her. I'll see her before she goes off duty at five."

"Yes, ma'am," agreed Sergeant Marlow.

"In the meantime try and get things running as smoothly as you can but if there's any trouble, just call me. That's all for now."

"Thank you, ma'am."

It was around four o'clock when Robert called on the ward again with some results from the lab which he had collected personally. He was in a much better mood, and the question of the medicine was not mentioned between them.

"I thought I'd slip along to Mrs. Edwin and give her some good news. Her lungs are clear, so she can go home as soon as her husband can get up from Osnabrück to collect her. We could arrange transport, but the corporal told me that he would prefer to come and collect her personally. His CO has agreed to give him time off. Has she any visitors now?"

"No, not at the moment anyway." Sophie felt much calmer now, and decided that she did owe Robert an apology. "I'm sorry you were involved in the trouble over the medicine today. Nothing serious could have happened because the juniors never give out any drugs or special medicines. They only serve routine ones."

"Well, there's no damage done and I presume you've dealt with the young lady responsible. Maybe this mistake will make your young nurse more careful in the future." He gave a low chuckle. "Don't look so glum, the world's not coming to an end yet."

Sophie could not help smiling, and her heart lifted. She wasn't sure how she had thought Robert would react this time, but he was being very nice about it. He had every right to tear a strip off her if he felt strongly about it.

Sophie was off duty at five, but as Martin was away in Berlin doing a locum and she was not going anywhere, she decided to have her talk with Rosemary Allen before she left the ward. Something had to be done about her, and it was no good putting it off.

"You wanted me, Sister?" Rosemary asked when she was sent for.

"Yes, Nurse, and what I have to say is between us, so please close the door behind you."

Despite her annoyance Sophie had difficulty in suppressing a smile when she saw the look of apprehension on the girl's face. It was a pretty face though with a certain precociousness about it that could be most irritating. She certainly looked much more attractive without the heavy make-up she affected when in mufti.

"I understand you've been teasing Helen rather a lot. Don't you think you've carried it a bit too far?"

"It was only in fun," replied Rosemary.

"I'm going to be frank with you and it's up to you how far the whole thing goes. If you'd like to transfer to another ward after our talk, I'll raise no objection. I have no complaint about your work; you are intelligent, you work hard, but you do lack a certain sensitivity as far as your colleagues are concerned. You create trouble among the juniors, but whether you do it deliberately I'm not sure. However, it must stop. Today you have been directly responsible for something that could have had very serious consequences."

"Who said so?" The question was full of surprise, not rudeness as the words conveyed.

"No one said so. I've eyes and ears and can see and hear for myself. I've been watching you for several days now, and I've come to the conclusion that you lack the *espirit de corps* that is so important to us all. If you lack that team spirit it can only prove to be a discordant note."

"Yes, ma'am."

"Remember, we're all members of *one* team, each dependent on the other to do the best we can for a smooth and efficient ward. Without that spirit one member can be like a bruise on a peach, once there it soon spreads and rots the whole fruit."

"Yes, ma'am. I'm sorry, ma'am." Sophie saw tears brighten the green eyes watching her.

"Why do you do it? Are you unhappy on this ward?"

"No, ma'am. I like it here. I guess it's just *me*. I'm jealous, I don't mean jealous in the usual way but when I hear Helen talking about her Mum and Dad something comes over me and I want to hurt her."

"But why? Have you no parents of your own?"

There was a look of pain on the girl's face, then two tears overflowed down her cheeks but she swallowed hard and soon had herself under control. It was only then that she answered.

"Yes, ma'am, but my father left my mother when I was a baby and I've never really got on well with mum, so when I hear others talking about their parents and their homes I get sort of jealous."

"I'm sorry about your parents," Sophie said sincerely, "but that's no excuse. I've known people who have had far less happy circumstances to cope with, but they don't allow it to affect their lives outside their homes. It's up to you to rise above such unfortunate circumstances. Learn to accept people who may be happier than you, but remember they can give you much more than you can give them. We can't choose our parents but we can choose our friends. Remember, I'm always available if anything worries you or you have a problem and need help. You only have to ask."

"Yes, ma'am. Thank you, ma'am. I'll try not to be bitchy in future."

"Good! Now you'd better get on with your work but, if you would like to transfer to another ward let me know."

"Please, ma'am, I'd like to stay here with you if you'll have me."

Sophie smiled at the nervous-looking girl who was twisting her fingers together. A smile altered the whole of the nurse's appearance as she said, "I'll try and do my best, I really will."

The following Saturday was the night Sophie was dining in the RAMC Mess as Robert's guest. It was the first time she had worn mess kit at Radlau. In the long, silver-grey dress with the scarlet roll collar she looked a little taller than usual, a fact which pleased her very much. She had always longed to be tall and willowy. She was willowy but anything but tall. She was "sawn-off" as Martin sometimes called her when he was in a teasing mood. It was the first time also that Sophie had seen Robert in his mess kit and she could not help thinking how handsome he looked in it.

In the entrance hall and in the anteroom where pre-dinner drinks were served, large bowls of flowers were scattered at several strategic points. When, escorted by Robert, Sophie first saw the dining room, she let out an involuntary, "Oh! It's beautiful," then stood there gazing at it all.

Along the full length of the table narrow bowls trailed soft greenery and scarlet carnations. On its highly polished red-brown surface their reflection was beautiful, creating a riot of colour, and edging the light on the crystal and silverware in flame and green. Interspersing the floral decorations, tall candelabra held matching red candles that flickered a soft warm light that was most flattering to the ladies.

"It's beautiful," she spoke softly.

"And so are you. I've never seen you looking lovelier."

A wave of happiness engulfed Sophie and she smiled

at Robert. Surprise at his unusual flattery kept her silent apart from a murmured "Thank you", but the glow of pleasure remained with her for the rest of the evening, sharpening her wit and colouring her conversation.

All through the soup, the grilled trout served with a delicious sauce, and the Mexican chicken, she divided her attention between Robert on her left and a captain who had just arrived at the hospital on her right. He was a nice young man, but Sophie found it difficult to draw him out. She was not sure if he was just shy or if he was normally a non-talker.

The sweet was a magnificent gâteau, one that only the Germans could produce. It was made of sponge cake cut into several layers and filled with fresh cream, strawberries and grated walnuts, and the centre, which had been cut out, was filled with ice cream in which fruit, nuts and brandy had been mixed.

"I'll have to diet to balance this," Sophie said laughingly to her host.

"Rubbish! You have a perfect figure. One meal like this isn't going to alter it now."

"It's nice of you to say so, Robert, but I can't take any chances. Besides, I couldn't afford to buy new uniforms. I've just bought a supply before I came out here."

"I suppose that's something to be reckoned with these days," he agreed.

When they had drunk a toast to the Queen, Robert offered Sophie a cigarette. Although she rarely smoked, this evening it seemed right that she should do so. On Robert's part, his offer had been nothing more than a courtesy gesture, and his look of surprise when she took one made Sophie laugh.

"Don't say it, but after that superb meal it seemed

right to have one and it's a perfect complement to this port. It's been a delicious meal and, Robert, thank you so much for inviting me. It's been a lovely evening."

"Glad you're enjoying it, but it isn't ended yet. There's to be some dancing after coffee."

"I'll enjoy that."

By the time the evening drew to its close Sophie was thoroughly relaxed and happy. She had danced most of the dances partnered by Robert, with the exception of one with the senior consultant, James Witherspoon, and one with the young officer who had sat next to her at dinner. When the evening ended she was quite disappointed, but told herself it was always better to end when you were enjoying yourself than to have to hang on for politeness.

Outside the sky was clear and the stars glittered like sequins. In a minor key, frost spattered the world around them and crackled under their feet as they walked the short distance to Robert's car. Without thinking Sophie suggested,

"If it's not too cold I'd like to walk back to our Mess."

"That's fine with me. I usually like to walk before I go to bed but wrap that scarf around your head and neck. I don't want you getting a cold." He was about to say something else but hesitated, then obviously changed his words. "What would Medical do without its sister?" Then he took her arm and they started off.

Outside the QA Mess Robert drew her into his arms. As he did so Sophie felt a sudden quickening of her pulse, and the full realisation that she was even more in love with this man. She tried hard to dismiss the thought, but when his lips covered hers she knew it was true. Unwilling to reveal her feelings she made a gesture of withdrawal, though she still hoped that he would not let her go. But with one of his lightning changes he released her, and with an almost curt "goodnight" left her without even giving her a chance to thank him for the evening.

"Good night and thank you, Robert," she called, but could not be sure if he had heard her.

It was about a week later that Joyce told Sophie during a conversation, "I don't know what you said to Rosemary Allen but she's a changed girl, and what's even more important, she and young Helen are growing quite friendly. I heard them discussing a dance in the guards' barracks, and Helen actually invited her to join in a foursome with some pal of her boy friend's."

"I'm delighted to hear it. It certainly appears to have made a difference to the atmosphere in the ward."

January, which had been quite mild except for a few bouts of exceptionally strong winds, went out without fuss, but February soon made itself felt with a spell of intense cold followed by heavy snow falls. Everywhere the earth lay covered by a thick carpet of whiteness. The branches of the trees were weighed down with the weight of the snow and the birds in Joyce's garden sat around the small outdoor patio, hoping for food.

Martin returned to Radlau in mid February. He telephoned Sophie immediately and invited her out to supper. Hurt, and faintly bewildered by Robert's change of heart and his cool aloofness ever since the night of the dinner, she accepted with alacrity. They went to the pub in the village where they enjoyed a pleasant evening.

"Did you miss me, love?" Martin asked when they were drinking their coffee.

"I did, very much."

"I bet not as much as I missed you. Oh, Sophie, if only you could have been with me in Berlin! It's a fabulous place. If Berlin is the result of losing a war, I hope next time I'll be on the losing side. And money, there seems to be lots of it around."

"I'd like to go some time while I'm serving here in Germany," she confessed.

"Maybe we could go together?"

"Maybe."

"By the way, did you know that Robert Austin won't be going with the skiing party in February? He's going to a conference somewhere at home for three days. I'm taking his place for the skiing. You're going, aren't you?"

"Yes, but has a definite date been made yet?"

"I believe it's to be the last Friday in February, but the numbers have dwindled a bit. There are only six or seven going now. That includes Gwen and Barry from the garrison battalion, Sister Vera from Orthopaedic and Ross Whittle from Gynae, and of course, you and me. By the way, there's an instructor at the resort if you want one – or perhaps you don't need tuition."

"I think one can always learn something no matter how proficient one may be, don't you? I certainly feel I can. What about accommodation?"

"The army will lay that on," Martin assured her. "There are chalêts and messes of a sort. I've been there once and found it most comfortable and there's a good supply of equipment if you haven't any. Ross has already made a provisional booking for us."

"I have no skis with me, but I've my own boots. That's something I think is much more important than anything else."

"Okay, see you tonight. There's a good film on. Does that sound okay?"

"That's fine," she said, "I feel like a visit to the cinema."

Sophie got her week's leave and, though she was sorry Robert would not be there, she was looking forward to skiing again. It was a sport she enjoyed. The instructor she had worked under in Scotland had told her she was a natural skier and she had learned quickly, but now she needed practice and she looked forward to the gorgeous feeling of rushing through the air as though on wings and the swish of the snow as the skis bit into it and sent it cascading away from her.

Just a few days before the party was due to leave for the slopes, Robert asked, "You're looking very gay this morning. Have you had some good news?"

"No, but I'm looking forward to the skiing holiday. I'm sorry you aren't coming."

He shrugged. "I'm sorry, too, but it's one of those things. This is a conference I can't refuse, even if I had that opportunity."

"Will you be able to visit your father and step-mother?"

"I doubt it," he answered with a tightening of his lips and a coldness in his voice that made Sophie wish she had never asked the question. But she could not help wondering what it was between Robert and his family that always made him react in this way. "Anyway, I'll be back on Tuesday," he concluded.

"Then you could come skiing part of the time."

"Would you like me to join the party?" he asked abruptly, sending a wave of embarrassment over Sophie but as she gazed at him there was a strange look in his eyes. Was it amusement or not? Whatever it was, she had the distinct impression that beneath that reserved exterior he was laughing at her. As for his joining the party, she had a strong wish that he would do just that, but all she said was,

"We'd all be pleased if you came."

CHAPTER SEVEN

THE morning the skiing party was due to leave Radlau was crisp, bright and sunny. Sophie drove with Martin and Ross Whittle from Gynae and Vera Baines, a QA who was joining her fiancé at the resort. Gwen and Barry Symons had gone ahead from Münster where Barry was stationed. Martin had to drive carefully because the roads were icy in places. Sophie was glad to be a passenger because she was free to look about her and enjoy the countryside, though it was not until they got nearer to the mountains that there was very much to see.

At ten they stopped at a *Konditorei* which had a small café attached. There they had coffee and a delicious slice each of coffee and walnut cheesecake.

"Have another piece," Martin implored Sophie, "you know how you love the stuff."

"I do, but one piece is quite enough. It would be sheer gluttony if I accepted another."

"Okay, then let's hit the road. I'm just dying to get on my skis and on the slopes."

"Have they any kind of ski-lift up there?" Sophie queried. Although she loved all aspects of skiing, she was always impatient to be at the top of the mountain coming down. The long hard climb upwards wasted too much time she always thought.

"Yes. Nothing sophisticated but it's quite efficient, once you know how to get on to the thing."

"And how do you get on?" Ross asked.

"Well, I just stand in the track of it, facing up the mountain, and when I feel the seat hit me behind the knees I just drop into it. Once you've done it, there's no problem. The thing is to relax immediately you feel the first touch of the cradle." He turned away and called, "*Kellner*, bill please."

"It's my do," Ross demanded. After a short argument Martin handed it over. Outside Sophie breathed deeply of the fresh and invigorating air.

The road after that began to climb and snaked through pine forests and open slopes covered with virgin snow. With the sun shining on it the scene was lovely, and Sophie longed to get out of the car and scoop the snow up in great armfuls or pattern the snow with tracks from her rubber-soled boots as she used to do when she was a child. She smiled to herself as she wondered what the others would think of such idiocy.

"Will we be able to do any skiing this afternoon?" she asked.

"Yes, most certainly, love. That's one of the reasons we left Radlau so early and ordered lunch at the camp. I can't wait to show off on the slopes. Incidentally there's a nursery slope there for beginners. Will you want to stay there?" Martin asked her.

"No, I think I can manage the runs."

"But that's super! Ross is pretty good, I know. Personally I can't wait." Quite unconsciously Martin revved the car to greater speed. It was much too fast for the conditions and taking a corner at the same speed, the car skidded on to a bank and wobbled for a minute or two. Sophie was sure it must turn over. Her main thought during these anxious moments was that whatever happened she must not make a fuss, but remain calm and with her senses well under control.

After that devastating interlude the car stabilised and stood balanced at about forty-five degrees. Martin, looking pale but composed, put the gear into reverse and edged slowly off the slope. Sophie kept her fingers crossed during the operation and hoped that there was no serious damage to the car. Once on the road again, Martin drew forward to a small indent at the side and got out to see if all was well. Ross and Sophie followed.

As far as they could see there was little damage. There were some scratches on the driver's side and the bumper had been slightly bent, but apart from that, there was nothing.

"Sorry about that, folks, but thank God it happened where it did and not there." He pointed ahead to where the side of the mountain fell away into a deep valley. "There it would have been curtains for us all."

"Our number isn't up yet, that's obvious, but would you like Sophie or me to take a turn at the wheel?" Ross asked kindly.

"No thanks. I'm all right now and I won't let that happen again, I promise."

From then on he drove more slowly than he had planned which made them half an hour late in arriving at the army ski centre. The rest of the party, who had left Radlau earlier than they had, were obviously worried and appeared to be greatly relieved when they saw the dark green Rover arrive.

After a quick lunch of goulash and *apfel strudel* they changed and met at the base of the ski lift carrying their skis and sticks which Susan and Barry had organised for them. Sophie was wearing tan ski trousers with a cream pullover and tan anorak. It matched the colour of her hair and Martin immediately nicknamed her "The Scarlet Runner".

At the top Sophie practised a few short runs, turns and stops then challenged Martin to a race down the mountain slope.

"You're on. Let's have five Deutschmarks on the race. Game?"

"That's okay by me, so," she turned to Ross, "will you count three to start us so that all's fair?"

At the count of three Martin shot away leaving Sophie trailing by a few feet but she soon caught up with him. The feel of the wind on her cheeks and the power of the skis beneath her was as heady as the best champagne. The actual race was forgotten as she leaned further forward into the wind and flew down the slopes, the snow spraying out on both sides in front of her like the sea from the bow of a fast speed boat. It was a glorious feeling, the only sound that of the wind and the swish of the skis in the powdery snow. It was not until half way down that she realised she had passed Martin and easing up a little she looked back. Martin was just picking himself up from the snow. Sophie waited to make sure that he was all right and had not hurt himself then turning again raced on through some trees and then out into the open again.

At the bottom of the slope she waited for Martin to catch her up. She felt marvellously well and happy and thoroughly satisfied with her achievement and glad she had not forgotten the art. Martin was only a few minutes behind. When he stopped with a great swishing of snow he complained,

"You've been holding out on me. You made me believe you were just a novice. How long have you actually been skiing?"

"About two years," Sophie told him, "mostly in Scotland which is not quite the same as here with the high mountains and the long runs. This is marvellous."

"You must be a born skier, that's all I can say," returned Martin.

"My instructor told me I was too, but did you hurt yourself when you fell?"

"No, only my pride. I was so busy watching you that I didn't look where I was going and hit a hidden boulder. You know, next time they hold army skiing championships you'll have to enter."

"No, I don't think so, I'm not a competitive type. I just like to do it for the fun."

"But if Radlau is represented and there's no one better, and at the moment there certainly isn't, it's your duty to try."

"Probably under those circumstances I might but I'd have to see. I've got a lot to learn yet," she said.

The following morning they went in a party with a guide for a full day's skiing across the mountains. It was a beautiful crisp morning with the early sun casting long shadows across the mountain side and setting the snow crystals glittering like cascading diamonds. Sophie, who loved all beautiful things, could only stand and stare until Martin nudged her arm.

"Come on, love. The guide is getting restive and we've a long day ahead of us."

"Sorry," she replied, "I was dreaming and admiring the beauty all around us, and it *is* beautiful, isn't it?"

"Yes, but let's get going." He turned and led the way. Sophie, adjusted her rucksack and joined the others who were getting in line to take the ski lift.

At the top of the lift the guide set off in a traverse around the mountain side, the others followed. Soon they were on the opposite side where the mountain was linked to the next peak by a wide ridge. Crossing this they climbed to the top of the new peak from which there was a most delightful view of the whole range, a serried expanse of peaks and valleys interlaced like the pattern of beautiful embroidery. Where the sun hit the snow it glittered and shone but the crevasses were like deep blue scores cut into the shimmering snow slopes.

"Come, we go now for *Mittagessen*," Hans, the German guide called. "There is a hut on the other side where we stop."

Once more the crocodile of skiers followed the track made by Hans. Sophie was third in line and going well though she was looking forward to the break as her legs were beginning to ache a little and she was ravenously hungry. It had been quite a long time since she had last skied.

The hut was just a small wooden construction which was planned for nothing more or less than protection for anyone caught in a blizzard or bad weather conditions. There were bunks built along three sides of the building on which the skiers perched to eat their packed lunches.

"You're looking very bonny," Ross Whittle told Sophie, "like the traditional English rose with your red cheeks." He turned to Hans and asked, "What's the programme after this?"

"We traverse down the other side of this mountain to the valley where there's a *Gasthaus*. We have coffee there and then take the lift up the next mountain and then ski down to the lower slopes, and from there to the camp. I hope you all enjoy today?"

It was Sophie who answered first. "It's been marvellous. I'd forgotten how exciting skiing on open places could be. Thank you, Hans."

"*Bitte, Fräulein!* It is for me a great pleasure."

"Hans, join us at the party tonight." It was Martin who spoke now. "I understand there's to be a dance. Do outsiders come too?"

"Outsiders?" Hans looked baffled.

"Strangers."

"Ah! Strangers, yes. Plenty people come from along the valley, but now we go, ha?"

The run back was just as enjoyable but by the time the camp came into sight Sophie knew she couldn't have gone much further. How she was going to dance she had no idea but she was looking forward to the evening, nevertheless. Momentarily she wished that Robert had been able to come. Anyway, she hoped he might turn up for the last couple of days.

"Having a good time?" Martin asked her as they bent to remove their skis.

"Marvellous!" she answered. "Apart from the joy of the exercise I love being among mountains and hills. That's the only drawback to Bollingham for me. It and Hull and the surrounding countryside are too flat, although we are not far from the Wolds. It's like Westphalia, for that matter. I think I'd like to live in a nice spacious bungalow right up near the top of a hill or on the side of the mountain and where I could look over vast areas, woodland preferably."

"I'm a townie myself, I like the bright lights and the theatres and night clubs, but if you were with me, I'd settle for anything." He was silent for a few moments, then turning to Sophie he took her hands in his and asked with a greater solemnity than he had ever shown before, though she wasn't sure whether it was assumed or serious,

"Will you marry me?"

Sophie suppressed a smile. She had received three proposals of marriage during her life but this was the most unromantic and the most unexpected of them all. Here among the clatter and chatter of the crowd, her nose red, and damp patches all over her clothes, it seemed quite incongruous, but knowing that Martin was not one who took kindly to being laughed at, she answered as seriously as she could.

"I'd like notice of that question and then I can get my breath back."

"If you say yes I won't try and rush you into it too quickly," he said. "I'd like to take my exams first. I'm due out of the army in three years' time and I hope to get every qualification I can before that date. I have great plans for my, I mean *our*, future."

"Martin! Please don't take me too much for granted. I like you very much but I don't think I'm in love with you and I have no intention of compromising. If and when I marry it must be to a man I love totally. I once thought I'd found that man when I became engaged to Doug, but as I told you the other evening, I was mistaken."

"Thanks for being so honest with me but is there anyone else around?" The question appeared on the surface to be a perfectly normal one, but Sophie could sense the intensity and the nervous apprehension behind it.

"No, there's no one else." As she spoke they reached the deserted entrance to the large chalet which served as the main building in which all the services including the dance floor were situated. She took Martin's face between her cold hands and kissed him gently on the lips, but when he would have taken her in his arms, she eluded him.

"Okay, love. I can hope at least." Then with a quick change of mood he added, "Meet you here in five minutes for a spot of schnapps, okay?"

"Okay."

The evening was one of the most enjoyable Sophie had spent since her arrival in Germany. After several modern dances, most of which she had with Martin, some of the German employees of the camp walked on to the floor. They were dressed in white shirts, grey lederhosen, long woollen socks and dark shoes, to perform a *Schuhplatler*. Hans was with them and appeared to be their leader. When the dance was finished and the enthusiastic applause died down, several of the men walked across to the girls watching and invited them to dance. Hans stood before Sophie.

"Please, Fraülein, will you dance with me? I teach you the *Schuhplatler*. It is a Bavarian dance."

She was about to refuse but knew it would be ungracious to do so. Reluctantly she took his outstretched hand and walked with him to the centre of the floor. Before the music began each man demonstrated a few of the steps to his partner.

The dance was not so much complicated as it was difficult to get into the rhythm of it. After a few false starts Sophie managed to master the steps and actually began to enjoy the dance. When it ended the applause was deafening.

"Good show!" someone roared from the crowd and Hans bowed low to her, taking her hand, kissed it. "You are very good, Fraülein. You learn quickly."

"Thank you. You're a good teacher and Hans, thank you for the run today. It was really marvellous."

He beamed. "That is good, Fraülein. Thank you. We go tomorrow the other way. You will come?"

"I hope so, if my muscles are all right. They're feeling tired and I've found some I never even knew I had."

"Have a good hot bath tonight and massage your legs and tomorrow you will be fine."

"I'll do that. Thanks for the advice."

It was almost midnight when the dancing stopped. Hot soup was then brought in with thick chunks of fresh bread and butter. It was delicious and was appreciated by everyone despite the near exhaustion some of them were suffering, Sophie among them.

"Like to come for a quick walk before bed?" Martin asked.

"Sorry, but I really couldn't walk another step if I aim to go skiing tomorrow," she said wryly.

"All right, love. You're right, of course, but dream about marrying me."

"I will. Goodnight. I'm glad I don't have to go out into the cold now. Still, you haven't far to go for your chalet, have you?"

"No more than a few yards. 'Night."

Sophie followed Hans' advice, but once in bed she was soon asleep. She was wakened by the morning sun edging its way around the slats of the shutters and creating chevrons of light across her face. She lay there for a few minutes enjoying the warmth and comfort of the thick quilt. Then throwing it off, she washed and dressed hurriedly for breakfast and another day of skiing.

It was at the top of the first mountain that someone in the party was overheard to say that he had listened to the news on his radio and that there had been warnings of avalanches. Hans confirmed the statement but added, "We do not have many serious ones in this area. It is usually in the higher mountains where they happen."

"Good! I'd hate not to be able to ski," Sophie told Martin. "I'm enjoying myself so much."

"So am I, love. I really am. Having you along has made the holiday perfect."

"Martin, you're very sweet." He was about to interrupt her and, guessing what he was about to say, Sophie forestalled him. "Don't let's get serious now. Let's just enjoy the week then we can talk about it again."

"All right, it's a bargain," and bending he kissed her quickly on the lips despite the rest of the party gathered round.

The day, still bright with sunshine was a little warmer than the previous one and the skiing followed the same pattern. At the top of the last mountain Hans pointed out the different directions.

"That way it is Berlin. There the Democratic Republic," then swinging around he pointed to the plain that was Westphalia.

Radlau seemed such a long way away and Sophia could hardly believe that she had been there only three days ago. She hoped her ward was running smoothly and that there were not too many crises. Her thoughts turned to Robert, and she wondered if he would arrive with the party expected that evening or on the morrow. She wasn't quite sure of the exact date. Hans called them and interrupted her thoughts, and pushing with her sticks she followed across the mountainside. It was just as they had completed the last climb that they heard a strange roaring sound. Sophie looked around, but could see no cause for the noise. Then she heard Hans' warning.

"Avalanche! *Achtung*! Keep close to me and ski as fast as you can. We cannot go down this side of the mountain because it is too dangerous. We must go round. Come!"

They had been skiing for about fifteen minutes when a roar from another direction came to their ears. This time it was much closer. In fact as far as Sophie could judge it was coming from the ridge just above them.

"*Schnell, schnell*!" Hans roared, forgetting in his distress that few of the party spoke German.

"Quick, quick," she translated for them. No one needed urging now. Each in his own way felt a deep fear surging through them. Sophie had never been quite so frightened in her life, thought she kept a tight hold on her emotions. If but one of them were to lose the grip on themselves there could be panic.

"Five minutes now and we all be safe." Hans reassured them just as the roar suddenly seemed very close and glancing up, Sophie saw a giant wall of snow descending towards them like a huge waterfall. Just for a moment she felt panic, then asserting her self control she pushed with her sticks in an effort to increase her speed. Martin, who had been ahead a few yards waited now for her to draw level.

"Don't wait for me, just keep going. I'm all right, Martin."

The fringe of the descending snow was now just above them and coming faster and faster. Sophie tried to speed up, but she was doing as much as she could without descending at a sharper angle. As it was she had veered slightly to the left of the track along what appeared to be good firm snow. She breathed a sigh of relief when she heard the main body of the snow fall behind her and she was still clear. The next moment she felt a sudden jerk of her skis and the whole of her body seemed to be enveloped in a wave of searing pain. Suddenly the whole world revolved around her and then she sank into oblivion.

CHAPTER EIGHT

Sophie had no idea how long she had been unconscious but it could not have been for more than a few minutes as she had not yet begun to feel cold. It took her a further few moments to realise what had happened and where she was. When full realisation did come, she felt a fear greater than she had ever known overwhelm her. It was then she began to tremble, due partly to the cold, but mainly because of her fear. Then, asserting control of her senses, she tried to take stock of her situation.

Yes, she was lying in the snow. Of that she was fully aware, and also that her face was near some sort of rock. Between it and her there was a tiny clear space which enabled her to breathe. The snow covering her seemed to weigh her down but she must try and do something to help herself, though her thoughts were still a little confused. She remembered the cascade of snow hitting her with great force, knocking her over and pushing her headlong down the mountainside for some considerable distance. Somewhere she had lost a ski and one of her sticks. The other she still had, because she could feel the leather thong caught around her wrist.

Tentatively she tried to move her legs, the left first. With a great effort she managed it at last, then she tried her right one, but to her great consternation she found that it was firmly wedged down by her ski, which in turn was held by some object she could not feel. She did not think there was any great injury to the leg itself except for a little pain in the ankle.

Next her arms. The right one was all right though

the movement was restricted by the snow, but the moment she tried to move the left one she knew it must be fractured. The pain was acute. She tried to cradle it in her right hand to enable her to turn her body which was in a half-twisted position, but the ski anchoring her leg prevented any movement. Keeping the rest of her body as immobile as possible she managed to release her hand from the ski stick and began scrabbling at the snow above her. She knew it was a hopeless task because as she moved some more fell in its place, but she was doing something. The fight for survival was on.

How long she had been trying to perform the impossible Sophie had no idea, but the cold was now having an effect; sapping all her energy and creating a mild amnesia as far as her situation was concerned. In a great effort to rally her full senses she tried to think of something. She began flexing her muscles one by one in the hope of keeping her circulation going. Then she had an idea. It would probably prove to be hopeless, but at least she would be trying.

Feeling for her ski-stick she managed to find it and to pull it inch by inch towards her shoulder. If she could push it up through the snow so that any rescue party, and she did not doubt that there was such a party, might see it.

While she worked she did not feel the cold quite so badly, but when she was forced back into a state of shivering inactivity, as she was from time to time, she was all too conscious of the chill fingers of frost creeping from her toes upwards and threatening to overwhelm her. As she grew physically weaker, so too did her will to fight. She began to feel desperately sleepy and had almost dozed off when some remaining shred of will power urged her to fight on. Ignoring the pain in her arm, and with a tremendous physical effort, she began clawing at the snow above her once more only this time with more desperation until a glimmer of her old intelligence warned her to pack the snow from below upwards, making the sides of her chimney to the fresh air firm. Then, quite suddenly, she saw the snow lighten just above her, just to the right of the stick's shaft. She pulled off her scarf and managed, with great difficulty, to free it from her neck. Withdrawing the stick she worked painfully and slowly to wind the scarf around the end of it. That done as best she could, she forced it through the snow where it had been loosened by her earlier attempts. At last she managed to penetrate the icy blanket above her.

Once through, she tried to create a larger opening by working the stick from side to side. At first it seemed to be a losing battle. As she displaced some of the snow fresh falls filled the space, but at last, when she knew she would soon have to give up, she managed to clear an aperture about a foot wide. For a few seconds she hardly dared breathe for fear of bringing another fall down on her, but the space remained. Taking several deep breaths of the cold but clean air, she began working feverishly to enlarge the aperture so that she might crawl out, but still more snow kept replacing it.

After what seemed hours Sophie was forced to lie still. She was physically exhausted, and her mind was in a state of turmoil interspersed by moments of resignation and utter despair. Sometimes her mind was a blank then thoughts began chasing each other across its surface. She forced her mind to act and concentrated her thoughts on Robert. Would he regret her loss when he heard about her death? Would he dismiss the news as another unfortunate case? No, he had too much compassion for that. Besides he was fond of her, of that she was quite sure. There had even been times when she thought he was falling in love with her. The significance of her thoughts brought new hope to her. If he was back from that conference in London he would already be on his way once the news reached Radlau.

With sudden clarity she knew that her love for him was both total and irrevocable. The knowledge gave fresh impetus to fight and once more she began digging at the snow but the effort was futile except that it kept her blood circulating. For what seemed like hours her mood swung from one extreme to the other. One minute she was filled with hope the next with self-pity and despair.

Nobody knew where she was lying. It could be at the bottom of some deep crevasse or hidden by an overhang of rockface. Terror gave her new courage and once again she tore at the snow with little success. She was growing rapidly weaker and the cold was creeping higher and higher along her body when a faint sound came to her, one that she could not identify. Now it was much nearer.

"Of course," she spoke aloud, her voice muffled by the snow packed around her. "A helicopter! Thank God." She began to wobble the stick once more, praying that it was visible from the air. Then desperation overtook her as the sound began to move away. They had not seen her despite the scarf! In that moment she knew the very depth of despair. The sudden surge of hope and then the snatching away of it was more than she could bear.

Sophie felt tears, the only warm thing she had experienced for what seemed like hours, trickle down her cheeks as the silence, so absolute, almost hurt in its intensity. How long the apathy lasted she could not determine, then she thought she heard voices, and listening with every nerve strained, she knew that somewhere near there were men. She tried to shout, but only a whisper emerged from her lips. "Please God, don't let them go away and leave me alone again." Then she knew the rescue party was digging her out. She recognised the voice of Hans the instructor. The other voices were those of strangers.

"Thank God!" she shouted but no shout came — then blessed relief when she heard Hans ask,

"Are you all right, Fräulein?"

Sophie tried to answer, but some of the snow falling closer around her muffled the sound and filled her mouth. Spitting it out, she cupped her hand as a shield above her lips and in a very weak voice, though she still thought she was shouting, she managed to answer.

"Yes, I'm here, Hans."

At last the snow was cleared off her and Hans and another instructor Sophie had seen on the slopes bent over her.

"Are you badly hurt anywhere?" the stranger asked.

"Only my arm," she said shakily. "It's fractured, but apart from bruising I don't think there's anything serious, except for the cold. I cannot feel anything in my feet or legs. They're quite numb now, and there's something across me, holding me down. I think it's my ski."

"Never mind, Fräulein. We'll soon have you free." Even as the man was speaking, he and Hans and someone Sophie could not see began clearing more snow away. When she was uncovered it only took a few seconds to remove the ski and lift her very gently from the ground and lay her carefully on to the narrow rescue stretcher. Sophie cradled the fractured arm until she was on the stretcher, then the men immobilised it with some lightweight splints they had brought with them in case of need. When she was safely strapped in and covered with blankets they signalled the helicopter, which was hovering not far away. As it flew into the immediate area Sophie asked Hans,

"The others of our party, are they . . . all right?"

"Yes, Fräulein. Dr. Moore has cracked his ribs and had his head cut badly, and Captain Symons had a broken finger. The others, they are all well and are back at the camp."

"I'm glad," said Sophie. "Things could have been much worse, couldn't they?"

"Yes, Fräluein, but now we must get you back too. It is lucky that you stopped on this wide ledge. A little further and it could have been very bad for you as the drop into the valley is very steep. Also the helicopter can land here to take you off." As he spoke the machine came down a few yards away from where the stretcher lay. The wind from the rotor blades threw snow in great cascades around them. Then the men bent and lifted her carefully from the ground, talking and encouraging her as they did so. Even in her pain Sophie was conscious of the kindness of these men and the dedication they must have to be ready to rescue people from accidents such as hers.

At last she was secured to the helicopter and she felt it lift into the air, swing sideways and then move off in a slightly downward motion towards the village and the camp. There willing hands took the stretcher from the machine and carried her into the Medical Centre where she was greeted warmly by the MO on duty.

"I hear you've been knocking yourself about. Anywhere else hurt besides your arm?"

"No. I feel as though I've been kicked by a mule or some such animal all over, but I'm sure there's no real damage. My legs and feet were numb, and though my toes haven't got back any of their feeling, my legs have."

"I'll give you something now to dull any pain then we'll get you into a nice warm bed while we get ready to set the arm."

"Thank you. You're all very kind." She was silent for a few moments as they moved her in to a blanketed bed with hot water bottles, then she asked, "I didn't thank Hans and his friend for rescuing me. Please can you get a message to them? Tell them I'd like to see them when they've rested and can spare the time. I'd like to thank them in person."

"I'll do just that," then turning to the corporal on duty he told him. "Go and find the instructors and give them Sister Allendale's message will you, Forbes?"

"Yes, sir." The corporal saluted smartly and hurried off.

The rest of that day and the ordeal through which she had gone were soon forgotten. She was dimly aware of people hovering near her bed and the weight of the plaster on her left arm, then sleep, glorious strength-making sleep, engulfed her and it was not until breakfast time the following morning that she became fully conscious.

For a few minutes she lay glorying in the warmth and comfort surrounding her, then she remembered her toes. Were they frostbitten? Almost too afraid to try, at last she made up her mind and with a determined effort at asserting her will power she began to move those on her right foot and then her left. They were all right. She felt relief surging through her.

"Good morning! And how do you feel this morning?"

"Fine, thank you," she told the captain who had seen to her the previous evening. "I've just been trying my toes because I was afraid of frostbite, but they seem all right now, thank goodness."

"Yes, we were a little apprehensive, but with gentle massage and warmth we got the circulation going again."

"Thank you. How are the others?"

"They recovered just as you have," the captain told her. "Your party was remarkably lucky. Others have not been quite so much so. A party of Germans from Hanover have lost two people. The search parties are still out, but as far as we know, there is still no sign of the missing couple, a man and his fiancée."

"Poor things! I can't help thinking how lucky I was. It could so easily have been fatal for me too."

The Captain smiled. "Well, never mind. Ah! Here's Sister Benedict with your breakfast. I hope you're hungry."

"I'm ravenous," answered Sophie.

"Good. Then I'll leave you in peace. Tomorrow you'll be going down to Radlau. You'll be more comfortable there."

"Thank you."

When she had eaten a good breakfast and had been settled down, again, her thoughts kept returning to Robert and the knowledge that she was in love with him. How was she going to hide that fact from him? It would need all her self-control to do so, she knew. Working with him and seeing him on the ward every day would be sheer misery.

She thought about asking for a transfer, but she had been in Germany for less than six months. It would not only look strange, but would be irresponsible for her to request such a thing for purely personal reasons. Besides she loved the work there, and she loved being in the country.

Her thoughts were interrupted by Ross Whittle who had escaped unhurt. "They've just been on the 'phone from Radlau; your parents are flying over to see you next Wednesday. They send you their love and a message that they're so glad you're all right now. When they heard the news they wanted to get a flight immediately to be with you, but Matron, to whom they apparently spoke, said that she would arrange a booking from Manchester for them. They arrive at Münster airfield some time Wednesday afternoon and your friend Captain Austin has volunteered to meet them there."

"Everyone is being so very kind," Sophie answered, tears threatening in her gratitude and the thought of Robert being so kind, but then that was typical of him and had no other significance. He would treat anyone who had been hurt with the same kind courtesy and compassion.

She closed her mind to thoughts of Robert and concentrated on her parents and their forthcoming visit. Her longing to see them and to bask in the warmth of their love crowded out all other thoughts, bringing her a degree of comfort. It was fortunate that it was only her arm that was fractured! She would at least be able to get around and show them something of Germany.

That same evening news came that the body of the girl of the missing couple had been found, and that there was a full-scale search being organised to try and find the man. It was just possible that they might find him alive, but the hope was a forlorn one.

It was just after dark when Vera, the QA who had come with them, visited Sophie. "Hullo! How are you feeling now?"

"Fine thank you, and you?"

"Harry and I weren't involved really. We were way

ahead and so escaped completely. We certainly were the lucky ones. The teams are out searching now. You can see their torches from here."

"Will you pass me my dressing gown? I'd like to have a look, please."

"Are you allowed up?" asked Vera.

"To go to the bathroom and that sort of thing."

Vera helped Sophie drape it around her shoulders and walked with her to the window.

High up on the slopes they could see the naked flames of the torches creating a necklace of scarlet and gold as they traversed from side to side, then spread out like a fan to begin yet another traverse. For a few moments Sophie enjoyed the beauty of it, then she thought of the young engaged couple, one already dead, the other most likely so. Remembering her own ordeal, all the pleasure from the beauty of the scene left her and turning she walked slowly back to bed. It could quite well have been she they were searching for now, and that was a very sobering thought.

The following day Sophie arrived back in Radlau just after lunch and went straight to X-ray. From there she was taken to the Mess.

"There's no need to admit you into the ward," the duty officer told her. "You may just as well be comfortable in your own room with your things around you. I'm sure you'd prefer that."

"Thank you, yes."

Within minutes of arriving there visitors came rushing to see and welcome her back. She had no idea that she had so many friends. Ross Whittle, who had been luckier than the rest of the party and had escaped even the threat of injury because he had been well away from the path of the racing snow, came to see her. He had actually seen Sophie's bright tan figure caught and hurled down the mountainside, veering off to the right and around the side of the mountain. From his observations the rescue party had had some idea of the direction in which she must have finished up. Had it not been for him it might have been hours before she was found. There was little doubt in anyone's mind that she could not possibly have survived under those conditions.

"Well I must say it's good to see you looking so hale and hearty," he said. "And what a lovely tan you've acquired in such a short while. Three days ago I'd have given little hope for your chances. I guess God must have been taking care of you. I hear you've sustained nothing more severe than a broken arm, and a clean break at that."

"Yes, I was very lucky, very lucky indeed," agreed Sophie, "and Martin, have you heard when he's coming back to Radlau?"

"Tomorrow, I'm told, and he's fine. His fractured ribs have done no lung damage and the cut on his head turned out to be just superficial. Incidentally, he telephoned a few minutes ago to ask after you. I told him I'd ring back after I'd seen you in case you had any messages to send him."

"Thanks. Give him my love and tell him I'm looking forward to seeing him soon. And Ross, thank you for being so helpful over my rescue!"

"It was very little," he assured her. "All I can do is thank God that I turned at the right time to look if anyone was behind me. I must be off – I'm wanted in surgery. Anyway, I'll slip in and see you tomorrow. In the meantime, don't get dressed, but you can get up into a chair as long as you keep warm, and I *mean* warm."

"Thank you, sir," Sophie answered with a smile lighting up her features.

"I see we have the old Sophie back again. You must be feeling better."

A few minutes later Joyce came to see her.

"You're a nice one, going off to enjoy yourself and getting into this situation," she said, "but it's so nice to have you back and looking healthy after the ordeal of being buried under the snow as you were. I bet you felt pretty panicky at times."

"I did and I didn't, which is a contradiction of terms," replied Sophie. "The worst part of it was when I realised I was completely trapped and couldn't free myself. I tried some digging out with my free hand but it was rather exhausting. It got me nowhere, but let's not talk about it now. I'm okay, which is more than two other skiers are, poor things. Tell me about the ward. Any interesting admissions?" she asked, though what she really wanted to ask was, "How is Robert?"

"One or two, but nothing outside a routine pneumonia, a query gastric complaint and a patient for investigation. She's been stationed with her husband in Hong Kong and has some kind of fever, which hasn't been identified yet. They've taken some slides but the results aren't through." Joyce smiled at her friend before continuing, "The girls, non-nursing and the junior staff, all send their love and best wishes. Young Rosemary was quite upset when she first heard the news of your accident. You know, you've done a power of good where that young lady is concerned. She has settled down and gets on with the job just as well as the others. I think you've missed your vocation. You should be in the Diplomatic Corps."

Sophie laughed. "I'd be hopeless in that job." She looked momentarily embarrassed then asked, "How's Robert Austin?"

"The same as ever, imperturbable and polite, and

he asked after you. He didn't actually send you a message but he's coming to see you himself some time. He seemed genuinely concerned about you. I guess he knows what a damned good sister you are, and doesn't want to lose you from the ward."

"I should think more likely he was just being polite by asking after me, purely medical interest," said Sophie sadly.

"I don't know about that, but he was really upset when we first got the news about your accident. Of course he was still in England when it happened."

"Well, I'm glad to feel missed." Sophie smiled as she spoke, but her heartbeat quickened as she hugged the thought to her that Robert really had been moved by the accident.

"When do you expect to be back on duty?" Joyce asked.

"I'm not sure yet, but Ross has promised to discuss it tomorrow. I see no reason why I shouldn't be able to do light duties in a day or two. I'm afraid it will have to be light duties while I'm in this wretched plaster, but I'm sure there are plenty of things I can do."

"Well, don't rush it, Sophie. We can manage quite well at the moment, take care of yourself," said Joyce. "Clive asked after you and sends his salaams."

"Thanks! I was told that Robert had volunteered to meet my parents on Wednesday, that's the day after tomorrow. I seem to have lost count of the days. It's awfully kind of him. Will you thank him for me when you see him?"

"I will, but he'll no doubt visit you before then."

"Maybe," Sophie answered, her whole spirit lifting at the thought of seeing Robert again. It was at that moment that Oliver knocked at the door and came in.

"Your surgeon to see you, Sister," he announced, in

his most official manner. When the two sisters grinned at him he smiled, "Well, I heard voices and wasn't sure who the visitor was, so thought I'd best wear my official face and manner. It could have been Matron."

"It could have been, but it's me," Joyce chuckled.

Oliver turned to Sophie. "I've just been looking at your X-ray report. The setting is perfect and there are no complications of any kind. You shouldn't have any trouble with it. By the way, I've taken over from Ross so from now on *I'm* your Orthopaedic Consultant."

Sophie laughed. "Good! when can I be discharged?"

"Not for a few days at least. You'd be all right for light duties as far as the fracture is concerned but you've undergone a traumatic experience. You may feel all right, but you'll still have some physical reaction from the shock and the exposure. It will take a week at least to get over that. Anyway, your parents are arriving soon. You'll want some spare time to spend with them, so take all you can get. The hospital is pretty quiet at the moment – the 'flu seems to have died down and is on the wane throughout all the military stations. I believe in the civilian area it's dying out too."

When he had gone, Joyce suggested, "If you'd like it your parents could stay with me. I think they'd be more comfortable than in a Mess. Perhaps you could spend a few days with us too. How about it?"

"We couldn't put you to all that trouble," protested Sophie.

"It's no trouble. Clive and I would love to do it for you. Besides, I'd like your company when I'm off duty," declared Joyce.

"If you're really sure, I'd be delighted to accept, for myself and for Mum and Dad. You'll like them I know. They're very easy to get on with."

"If they're anything like you I'll not complain."

141

"Thanks, Joyce. I cannot tell you how grateful I am."

"Shucks! as an American friend of mine used to say. It's nothing."

The two sisters were joined by Clare who had just come off duty.

"Hullo, old thing!" she greeted her friend. "Hullo, Joyce. Sophie doesn't look as near to the point of death as I'd expected, but she is a little pale and interesting." She turned to Sophie. "I've missed having you around the Mess. I can't stay now as I'm meeting Oliver in twenty minutes' time but I'll look in when I get back tonight. I'll be quiet in case you're asleep. Take care of yourself," and throwing a kiss at her friends she hurried away.

"Clare certainly enjoys life, doesn't she, Joyce?" laughed Sophie.

"That's what being in love does for you. It looks serious. I wonder when they'll name the day? And what about you and Martin, are you thinking of getting engaged or anything?"

"No, not me. I'm very fond of Martin, but I don't honestly think I could love him enough to marry him, well, not as I feel at the moment anyway."

"Well, if you have any doubts, don't. I nearly made that mistake before I met Clive. I shudder to think what life might have been had I married George! Anyway, I must get home. Clive will be back early as he's taking me out to dinner in the village."

"Have a lovely time and give him my regards, please."

"I will, and we'll both look forward to having you to stay."

"Thanks a lot."

When Joyce had gone Sophie got out of bed and sitting before the dressing table mirror looked closely at herself. Apart from being a little pale her face appeared unchanged. With her good hand she brushed her hair well then applied some light eyeshadow and fresh lipstick in case Robert should arrive, but he didn't come until nearly six o'clock. He was accompanied by the senior sister who fussed around Sophie's bed, tidying the covers and plumping up her pillows. Robert stood, a little ill at ease, at the foot of the bed, though just in that first brief glance at him Sophie thought there was a gleam of pleasure in his eyes when he saw her.

"Glad to see you're recovering, Sister," were his first words, and spoken in his best official manner. "The ward misses you. Several of the patients have been asking how you are and when you'll be back, but I told them not immediately. I understand from Ross Whittle that everything is all right physically with you now. Glad the fracture was just a simple one."

"I'm glad too." Sophie, whose heart had been pumping madly since the moment of his arrival, settled back to normal again. She felt deflated by his cold official manner. How could I be in love with this man? she thought. It must have just been part of my nightmare. As for him, I doubt if he's capable of loving anyone. He's much too cold and dedicated to his work. He doesn't need people, not the way I do anyway. He's so self-contained, she decided. Remembering his offer to meet her parents she told him,

"It was very kind of you to offer to meet them, but surely the transport officer could arrange something for them? I can't drive like this," she indicated her plastered arm as it rested comfortably in its sling.

"No, that's quite unnecessary," said Robert crisply. "I offered to meet them and I'll do just that. If you're all right by then and Oliver, who I understand is

143

looking after you, agrees, there's no reason why you shouldn't come along for the ride – that is if you'd like to."

Sophie's heart began pumping away again at great speed. "That's kind of you," she said, "I'm sure Oliver won't stop me. I'd love to come. Thank you." Under her breath she added, "I'll see that he doesn't."

"I'll look forward to that." Momentarily his voice was gentle then the barrier was there again and with a brisk, "Good night. I hope you sleep well," he left her.

That night Sophie dreamed about him but it was an incoherent sort of dream. One minute she was held down by great snow heaps and he was trying to release her but as he cleared the snow away more snow fell and took its place. Then they were in a huge silver plane. she thought it was Concorde, flying over the North Sea. Robert was the pilot. She woke feeling a little tired but looking forward to the next day and her journey with him to Münster and the thought of seeing her parents.

CHAPTER NINE

THE sun was shining the following morning when Sophie was wakened by one of the members of the mess staff with her breakfast.

"There's a note from Captain Austin on your tray, Sister."

"Thank you." Sophie sat up, eager for the note but restrained herself until she was alone. It was merely to tell her that the plane was due at the airport at two-thirty and that he would call to collect her around one o'clock. If, however, she wasn't feeling well enough, or for some other reason preferred not to go, would she get a message to him?

Sophie had never felt better. As the day proceeded so her excitement grew. It was not entirely on Robert's behalf but also for her parents. The thought of being with them even for a few days was a very happy one. She wondered how they would react to Robert, and more important still, how he would react to them. She hoped they would like one another but so much depended on whether he relaxed with them or not. He would probably do so with her father because he had that rare quality of empathy that endeared him to people.

Sophie was ready and waiting in the anteroom at one o'clock, but she was so filled with excitement that she found it difficult to relax. Although she was feeling like her normal self once more, she found she tired very easily so she forced herself to sit as much as possible.

The dress she had chosen to wear was one of green

and cream small check, with a plain, darker shade of green collar and cuffs. The sleeves were wide enough to cover the plaster, provided she left the cuff undone. She knew it suited her well, a fact that was confirmed by Clare when she was helping Sophie to dress.

"I've never seen you look nicer *or* smarter. It really does something for you. I'm sure Robert will approve when he sees you. It would do that man good to get involved with someone like you."

"Amen to that," Sophie told herself. Aloud she answered,

"That will be the day."

"It will. By the way, I hear he's going to London to take another examination. I'm not sure if it's paediatrics or his obstetrics this time."

"When does he go?" asked Sophie.

"Next month some time. He's a clever fellow, isn't he?"

"He certainly is, and a very fine doctor too." Something in Sophie's voice must have interested Clare who turned to her now,

"You're not falling for him, are you?"

"No." The lie felt heavy on her tongue and she added quickly, "but I do like him despite his moods. D'you remember him at Joyce's Christmas party? He was so amusing and so entertaining. Sometimes on the ward now I can hardly believe they are one and the same man."

"No, I can't either but they are and when I first knew him he was always like that which, to my mind, seems an awful waste of a damned nice man."

"I couldn't agree more," but Sophie's idea of waste was a little different from Clare's.

It was precisely one o'clock when Robert was shown into the anteroom. Sophie stood up, her heart thumping as he came towards her. As she bent to pick up her camel coat he stopped her,

"Leave it. I'll help you."

Picking it up, he held it out for her to slip her good arm into it, then very carefully he placed it across her other shoulder and, turning her round, brought it as far as he could across the plaster cast on her left arm.

"I'm afraid it won't button," he said.

Robert did everything he could to make her comfortable. She had never felt quite so cherished or cared for, not even by Doug. Once assured that she was "beautifully warm, thank you," he helped her to the car. When he had taken her arm her first instinct had been to pull away but something someone had said to her once, she could not remember who, came to mind.

"All men like to have their ego boosted, especially by a girl they are interested in, and the best way to do that is to let them think they are taking care of the little woman." Perhaps this was where she had always gone wrong in the past, by asserting her independence with Robert.

The feel of his hand under her elbow set her pulses racing and gave her a lovely feeling of warmth and pleasure. It was very nice, being cared for in this way. She must remember and allow it to happen more often. She was even more impressed when, after she was sitting comfortably in the car, he placed a cushion, which he had brought especially for the purpose, on her lap to take the weight of the plaster from her neck. "Slings aren't the most comfortable things to wear."

Much of the snow had disappeared and in places was mushy underfoot, but the gardens made up for it. Many of them were garlanded in purple, yellow and white crocuses and late snowdrops. Clumps of blue scilla added more variety to the scene.

"They're beautiful aren't they?" asked Sophie, and Robert nodded.

"They are rather, Isn't it incredible that flowers as fragile as snowdrops can grow and survive in such cold weather? I'm always amazed by them."

"So am I. We have a large garden and several rockeries at home and the whole place is like some great work of art with spring flowers. Dad grows crocuses round the edges of the lawn and snowdrops under the trees, and they are really glorious."

"My father, though he hasn't time enough to actually garden himself, is very clever at planning. He has, or had, a full-time gardener and two old-age pensioners who came to help from time to time. I alway found it a little too well planned, too much like a public park display. I like things to be irregular as though they just grew, but perhaps that's as bad as over-planning."

"I think a little planning is necessary even for a natural garden otherwise it could become a wilderness. Dad seems to get the whole set out just right. At least I think so," she added hurriedly.

"I'm sure you're right," he agreed. "Anyway I welcome the colour here. It's not merely the lovely sight but it's the promise of things to come. Who knows what might be just around the corner?" With a flash of his natural wit he added, "Such as a dumping in the snow, though I'd prefer that you should choose something more gentle than an avalanche." She could hear the laughter in his voice and her own mood lightened. This was the Robert she loved most, and the part of him that was not seen often enough.

"If only he would stay this way and think of me as a woman and not just the sister-in-charge of his ward." She glanced sideways at his profile and decided she had never seen him quite so calm and friendly as he was at this moment. It was then that he turned his head too quickly for her to evade his blue eyes as they looked straight into hers. Normally she thought of them as the eyes of a thinker, but now there was some subtle change in their depths. What it was she could not determine, but of one thing she was sure. Today there was no hostility there as there sometimes had been in the past.

"You seem quite excited today," he said softly. "It suits you, makes your eyes sparkle and gives you more colour in your cheeks. Are you and your parents very close?"

"Yes, we always have been. And you?" She regretted the question the moment it was uttered when she saw the familiar tightening of his lips. He was silent for a few minutes then he answered reluctantly,

"I used to be, especially with my mother when she was alive. Even after that I had a reasonable association with my father, but things haven't been quite the same since he remarried." He lapsed into one of his moody silences, then, much to Sophie's surprise, he began speaking again.

"As you know, my father is a consultant gynaecologist and he wanted me to specialise in the same subject, but Gynae is not my line. If I ever were to specialise I would choose Paediatrics, but as I once told you, my real love is to get into a good group practice somewhere in Yorkshire, or I might even stay in the army. One thing I do *not* want is any connection with Harley Street."

"Well, from a security point of view the army is best," Sophie said. "You are part of something that really cares for its members and stands behind them when necessary. I've seen that with this accident. Had it happened when I'd been in civilian nursing, my immediate friends would have been kind and come to see me and done anything they could to help but here, among army people, everyone tries to do what they can in all kinds of little ways, and even more important, the higher powers are all interested in one's welfare. It gave me such a nice warm feeling. And look how good they are in flying relatives out when anyone, from the lowest-paid private soldier to the highest-ranking general, gets really ill. I can't see any civilian firm, well very few, doing that for their employees."

"Yes," agreed Robert, "I suppose being in the army is what one might even call being a member of a club. Ah! Here we are."

Although Robert's car was registered with a British Forces' number, both he and Sophie had to show their military passes before they were allowed into the airport. There they found that the plane was due in on scheduled time, in just twenty-five minutes.

"Let's find some coffee," Robert suggested, "or would you prefer tea?"

"Coffee, please."

As she sipped her steaming hot coffee Sophie had never felt so happy. In his present mood she could not ask for a nicer companion and even better, there had been a subtle change in their relationship. Had anyone asked of her what that relationship was, she would have answered, "True friends."

True friends! That had a nice ring to it. Looking up she saw Robert watching her closely. Then he spoke.

"You look like the cat that has just caught a nice fat mouse. May I ask what you're thinking about?"

"You," she blurted out and then regretted it. Thinking quickly she added, "and how kind you are to drive all this way for me and my family."

"That's what friends are for," he replied.

"Then are we friends?"

"I thought we were."

"Then we are." She smiled at him and his response was immediate. Just then there was an announcement that the plane from Gatwick was arriving in five minutes.

Robert paid the bill then hurried to her side to pull out her chair and help her up. "Let's get a place near the entrance then you can see them a little sooner."

Sophie, always nervous about flying, was tense until the plane actually arrived.

"There it is," Robert announced and looking in the direction he indicated, Sophie saw a shining silver speck as the spring sunshine caught part of the fuselage and one wing in its rays. She tried to relax when she realised just how tense she was, but it was not until the plane actually began to taxi towards the Arrivals building that she was able to do so completely.

Within minutes people were streaming down the mobile steps now placed against the plane. At last she saw her parents. Her father came first, every now and then turning to make sure her mother was all right. Both had small overnight cases. Men were already unloading the belly of the plane in which the heavy luggage had been stored. It was her father who saw her first and, waving, called to his wife who looked in the same direction and began to wave also.

Glancing at Robert, Sophie was embarrassed to find him watching her closely. There was a smile on his face of gentle amusement. For a few seconds she felt a mild resentment, then chided herself and smiled back to him as they moved closer to the customs post.

"There they are," In her excitement Sophie was not aware that she had grasped Robert's left arm.

"There's no mistaking your mother. You are both very much alike, though her hair has lost some of its fire." What he did not say was that there was a tranquility in the older woman's face that was lacking in her daughter's, but no doubt she would develop that as she grew older and more mature.

The next minute Sophie was enfolded in first her mother's then her father's arms, and she was kissing them unashamedly. The greetings over, her father held her away from him for a brief moment then said,

"Let me look at you. You're not showing any ill effects from the awful ordeal you've been through."

Sophie laughed. "I'm fine now, thanks, but let me introduce you to Robert. He's been so kind to me. Mum and Dad, this is Robert Austin." Even as she spoke there was a look of sadness in his face which for a moment puzzled her, then, remembering what he had said earlier about his father, it fell into place. He envied her.

"How do you do, Mrs. Allendale, Dr. Allendale. I hope you had a good flight?"

"Thank you. It was most comfortable, and we had a very friendly pilot who gave us lots of information as to where we were throughout the journey. My wife, who hates flying, said she really enjoyed this charter plane because the captain explained that there would be a change in the engine's sound as we began to descend."

"Yes, knowing what to expect made all the difference."

"It's a great pity they don't all do it." Robert took the case from Mrs. Allendale's hand and the heavy case that had been with the baggage from her father. "If you'll follow me, we'll load this into the car and be off."

Although she desperately wanted to sit beside Robert, Sophie insisted on her father sitting in the front.

"You can tell him about the countryside as we pass through. I don't know this part of Germany."

By the time they got to Radlau, Robert and her father had formed a friendly relationship that made Sophie very happy. The younger man had gone more than halfway in creating this condition so why, when he was with her, could he not act in the same way? Perhaps, she pondered, it was just that he didn't like women very much. There must be some reason for his extraordinary behaviour.

"Have you booked us into a hotel?" the older medical man asked of his daughter.

"No, you're staying with some friends of mine, Joyce and Clive Carey. I'm sleeping there too during your stay. Joyce is deputy on my ward."

"That's extremely kind of them! I hope we won't be a bother."

"I know you won't," assured Sophie.

"And you, are you still living in the Mess or have you taken private accommodation?" her mother asked.

"I'm in the Mess, and I propose to stay there. It's most comfortable and we're looked after very well. I'm not going to bother about finding somewhere else. Joyce is married to an infantry officer, so she has married quarters. It's an extremely good quarter with several rooms and plenty of space. I haven't seen their garden since the bulbs blossomed, so I should imagine it's quite a picture now. Joyce told me that the officer and his wife who had the place before them were very keen gardeners and spent much of their free time working in it."

Joyce who knew she would probably still be on duty when they arrived, had given Sophie the key and told her which rooms she had prepared for her guests. She herself would be free at five. Robert carried the cases up to their room and when he came down Sophie asked him if he would like some tea. "Joyce insisted that we should have some as soon as we arrived. Everything but the water is ready for us."

"Thanks, I would like a cup but I'll see to it. I know where everything is. I often come across here when I'm fed up with study or my own company."

This information surprised her. She had thought he spent all his spare time in the Mess. She remembered now Joyce saying on the odd occasion that Robert had been to see them, but she had merely thought it had no significance. Goodness! she thought, I am learning things about him today. More than I knew after seeing him for months.

"All right," she answered, "I'll just slip up and see if my folks need anything."

"Sophie," he called her back, "I like your parents very much. They're what I call real people. I can understand why you're so proud of them."

On the impulse of the moment she stood on her toes and kissed him on the cheek: the next moment she was in his arms and his lips covered hers in a long and hungry kiss. Then just as suddenly he released her.

"I'm sorry, I shouldn't have done that." Then he turned away and disappeared into the kitchen leaving her full of longing and bewilderment. Had it been a genuine desire to kiss *her*, or was it just an impulse that might have happened whatever girl he had been with? She had no idea. Her feelings in a turmoil, she turned and hurried upstairs to her parents' room. Crossing to her mother, she kissed her and then her father. Her father, who was a very discerning man, asked,

"What's up, poppet? You seem sort of agitated."

"No, there's nothing," she said. "I'm happy to have you both here. It seems years since we were together. Exactly how long are you staying?"

"Just a week. I've got a young man doing locum for me, but he's booked after that with a Hull practice."

"Well, a week is better than nothing. I have a week off so I'll be able to show you around. The only thing is that I can't drive with my arm like this, but we may be able to arrange with our transport officer for you to drive my car. Normally you have to have a British Forces special licence. How do you like Robert?" she asked, switching rapidly from one subject to the other.

"Very nice-looking, and a most charming young man," her father spoke for both parents. "And you, is he your special boy friend?"

"No, just a friend and the MO on my ward."

"Really?" her father quizzed her, but she knew by the expression on his fact that he knew that to her, Robert was more than just a friend.

When Joyce arrived home, followed soon afterwards by Clive, there was no doubt that everyone was going to get on well together. Sophie was delighted when Joyce insisted on Robert staying to supper that evening. It was a pleasant and happy evening for everyone. Robert had never been so friendly as he was now, and when Sophie suddenly remembered she had not brought her suitcase with her night things in it, he was the first to volunteer to collect it.

"You mustn't bother. I can slip across and get it," she insisted. "It's only a small case, so I'll have no difficulty in carrying it."

"Young lady, you'll do as you're told, and you're not walking over to the Mess either. I'll drive you and bring you back."

Again came the habit of years, a bid for her independence, then remembering her reactions earlier she accepted his offer as graciously as she knew how. Her answer obviously pleased him, and she felt she had scored a moral victory.

"Let's slip along now before everyone settles down. Where's your coat, upstairs or in the downstairs cupboard?"

"Downstairs."

"I'll fetch it."

Sophie, looking at Joyce at that moment, was interested in the expression of surprise on her face. Then Joyce gave Sophie a nod and a look which conveyed the message, "Now what's happening?" Sophie even began to hope that Robert might like her more than she had thought possible, but perhaps that was only wishful thinking.

When Sophie was safely settled in the car and Robert had taken his place at the wheel, he turned to her and asked,

"It's my free weekend. Would you and your parents like to come sightseeing on Saturday and Sunday? It would be a pity if they had to go back without seeing something of the country and I'd like to take you to see the Möhne Dam and the Jaeger Wald. They should both be looking rather lovely at the moment. What do you say?"

"Say? I'd love to come and I'm sure Mum and Dad would like to go too. It's very kind of you. Thank you."

"Good. Perhaps Clive and Joyce would like to join us but we'd need to take two cars then."

"That would be fun but I'm not sure if Joyce will be free. We can ask when we get back."

At the Mess Sophie felt she was floating on air as she went to her room to get her case. Robert was waiting at the bottom of the stairs to take it from her. His smile made her heart lurch and her hopes for the future soared into a new contentment.

Joyce was not off that weekend and so they were unable to accept Robert's invitation but she and Clive did accept Sophie's father's invitation to have dinner with him on the Saturday evening.

"It's a very small way of saying thank you, Joyce," the older doctor explained, "apart from the fact that I'd like to take you and your husband for a pleasant evening. I hope you'll come too, Robert?"

"Thank you, I'd be delighted," Robert assured him.

"Good! And can I depend on you to advise me as to the best place to go?"

"Certainly, and I'd suggest the Dalmatian in Münster. I know it's a long drive, but well worth it. If you agree I'll book a table for us."

"Yes please. I'd be most grateful."

Robert beamed with pleasure and answered without hesitation,

"Thank you, I'll certainly see to that. We'll have lunch near the dam, so if we leave here early there'll be no rush. Would nine-thirty be too early?" he asked Sophie, then turned to her parents. All agreed it was fine.

When Robert had gone and Sophie's parents had gone ahead to get ready for bed, Joyce asked Sophie, "What's going on with Robert? I think he's fallen for you in a big way."

"No, nothing like that. He's just in a good mood and treats me as a patient."

"There's more to it than that, but how do you feel? And what about Martin?"

"Martin and I are just good friends. He did ask me to marry him but I turned him down. I'm fond of him, but that's not enough for marriage."

"Stick to that philosophy if you want a truly happy marriage," Joyce told her. "I think you and Robert would be perfect together."

Sophie thought so too, but did not say it.

That week was the happiest since her arrival in Germany. She felt so cherished and content. Not only did she have her loving parents around her but Robert lavished every possible care and attention on her. Even more pleasing was that he spent all his spare time with her and her parents.

On Saturday morning they left for the Möhne Dam just after nine-thirty. Everywhere the fields and gardens were green with new growth, giving promise of spring.

The dam was much larger than Sophie had imagined it would be. The water reflecting the sky was a deep blue and hardly a ripple marred its silk-like surface. Along the banks, trees from lime colour to darkest green covered the slopes and duplicated themselves in the mirrored surface. This colour-drenched part of Germany, Sophie decided as Robert led them across the bridge, is truly beautiful.

When they arrived near the large object Sophie thought it looked precisely like the half of a space ship, she could not believe that it was what Robert told her it was. It was immense, and certainly had not the slightest appearance of a bomb to her mind.

"And that's only the lower half. With the two halves together how on earth could any plane carry such a weight?"

"I don't know the mechanics of it, but I assure you it's one of the bombs the Dambusters used."

While Sophie and her mother walked a little further along the bank, Robert and her father discussed some of the scientific aspects of this huge weapon, but when the two women rejoined them Robert suggested lunch at a village not far from Möhne.

As they knew they were likely to have a huge meal

that evening they all chose a light lunch. On the journey back to Radlau, Robert took them to a wooded area which was a nature park for a short walk. Pine needles carpeted the sun-dappled paths. The breeze, blowing gently through the cloisters of pines, created a symphony of sweet sound that brought even greater joy into Sophie's life.

"We'll just go to the top of this hill, then I think that will be enough walking for one day," said Robert. "But this view is something you must not miss."

Although Sophie was feeling desperately tired now, she climbed uncomplainingly to the top and was well rewarded. Through the trees and bushes she was looking down into a lush green valley. Cradled there was a village, many of the houses with red roofs. The church, of typical German architecture, was the focal point. Its spire, tall, slim and very straight, thrust upwards into the sky as though it served as a lookout for the people living below.

It was Robert who broke the spell.

"We should be getting on our way if we're going out this evening. We're quite a good way from Radlau still."

"Sorry," she smiled, "I was so enthralled by that view I forgot all about the time."

"Never mind. We'll make it."

At the Careys' Robert was persuaded to have a cup of tea before he went back to the Mess to change into more formal clothes. Sophie went with him to the door.

"Thank you, Robert, for a marvellous day. I know Mum and Dad enjoyed it too."

"Well, the day's not over yet. We still have tonight, and there's tomorrow."

Then quite unexpectedly he took hold of Sophie's hand, and pulling her towards him, he kissed her gently, but released her immediately and hurried towards his car, leaving her with a bounding heart full of joy.

For the rest of that weekend Sophie was in a seventh heaven. Although Robert had not said anything she felt sure he was growing fond of her. Beyond that she dared not think, but there was hope in her heart.

"What a charming man your friend Robert is," her father said while they were waiting for him to take them to the Dalmatian.

"I'm glad you like him," she answered. "He certainly appears to like you and Mum very much, and I'm glad. He can be a withdrawn sort of man at times."

"Robert withdrawn? I can't believe it."

"He can be. Ask any of my colleagues. He's also a very dedicated doctor, and a good one," she ended proudly.

"And you would like to be the doctor's wife?"

"Dad, don't say such things! There's nothing like that between us."

"Isn't there? I would have thought just the opposite, but maybe I'm mistaken."

On the Monday Martin came to see Sophie. He seemed very put out about something, and when Sophie asked him what was the matter he looked sulky then blurted out,

"I've hardly seen you since your parents arrived. Every time I ask you to come out you tell me you've already made arrangements with Robert Austin."

"I'm sorry, Martin, but it just happened that way because he drove me to the airport to meet them. We more or less made the arrangements then."

"Well what about dinner tonight? We could go to the village if you want a quiet evening."

Sophie was about to refuse, but changed her mind

when she saw the disappointed look on Martin's face. After all they were friends and he had been very good to her. Because she had fallen in love with another man did not mean she had to give up all her other friends. Besides, it was time she was honest with him and told him she could never marry him. She owed him that much. Even if her friendship with Robert never got any further than just that, she knew she still could not marry Martin.

"All right, if we can go to the village and have supper," she said.

"Okay. I'll call for you around seven."

CHAPTER TEN

THROUGH the magical beauty of spring to the colour-drenched gardens and warm caressing sun of early summer, Sophie's friendship with Robert grew into something very precious. Life was good. Robert had not spoken the word love between them, but she knew he was growing more and more fond of her and there were times when she felt really hopeful for the future. These were the evenings when his guard was down to reveal the gentle and delightful person he was underneath that withdrawn façade. But there were still times when the barrier returned and once more her happiness would turn to despair.

Thinking about the strange effect this man had on her, she felt deep rebellion building up within her. Why should she allow him to spoil her life? Why shouldn't she accept the many invitations to go out and enjoy herself? Well, from now on she would accept them but she was never able to relax enough to enjoy them as she used to. Besides it only appeared to alienate Robert more with the result that they saw less and less of each other off duty. In her heart Sophie was fully aware of Robert's disapproval and also knew that she was probably over-dramatizing the situation but something within herself kept driving her on.

On the ward it was quite different. There she managed to maintain a calm exterior, responding to his cold courtesy in like manner and always working with him for the good of the patients. Only once had she almost betrayed herself when she passed him some reports and their fingers touched. Her hand began to tremble and she thrust it quickly into her pocket to hide the movement.

But despite these moments of despair, and her desire to hurt him at parties she was always sorry afterwards because it was spoiling their friendship and that was something she valued.

Then came the evening when she, with all the Sisters who were free, were invited to a drinks party in the RAMC Officers' Mess. It was a most pleasant evening and Robert a perfect host. When he invited her to have supper in the village with him she accepted without hesitation but in a formally polite manner.

It was a glorious night with scarcely a cloud to be seen. The air was heavy with the perfume of flowers, some of which Sophie recognised, others that were strange to her. A full moon, set against a brilliant galaxy of stars, outshone the most elaborate setting of any old Hollywood musical.

It was just after leaving the *Gasthaus* where they had eaten that they saw a middle-aged woman half sitting, half lying on the pavement and just within the circle of light cast by the overhead street light. Robert drew into the kerb and jumped from the car, followed quickly by Sophie.

The woman was a typical German *hausfrau*. Her greying hair pulled severely back from a wide forehead did nothing for the pale drawn face with the blue pain-filled eyes. Robert greeted her in German, then asked in English,

"Are you hurt, Frau Mittelmeyer, or is it another heart attack?"

"It is the heart, and I 'ave forgotten my tablets," was the reply.

"You know you should never go anywhere without them, but my friend and I will get you home quickly.

Miss Allendale is a *krankenschwester* who works with me at the hospital."

As they helped the woman to her feet and carried her in a hand cradle to the car, she told Sophie, "Herr Robert is a very good friend. He help me many times. But for him I die."

Sophie smiled at her, then glanced at Robert. As she had expected he was embarrassed and, when he spoke, his stammer was much worse than usual. That, and the infinite look of compassion on his face, made Sophie's heart swell with love and pride for this man who was so full of humility. He would never volunteer any information on such things, as she was already aware. His reply now was typical of him.

"It was just lucky that I happened to be around when you had that initial attack, but no more talking. Relax as much as you can."

The house to which Robert drove them was a neat, two-storey one painted in pale green with a neat garden and lawn in front and around it. Inside the house it was meticulously clean as Sophie had expected it would be. Robert introduced her to Herr Mittelmeyer and his sister-in-law, Frau Eva Holtz. There was no doubt of their deep concern for the sick woman as they greeted Robert with great warmth.

Inside they were ushered into a room on the left side of the passage. Sophie noticed a bottle of tablets and a carafe of water on a small side table. Herr Mittelmeyer passed the tablets and a glass of water to Robert as soon as his wife was settled in the chair.

"Once again you have come to our help, Robert." The German held out his hand and grasped Robert's firmly. "And you, Fräulein, thank you, too."

It was Robert who replied for both of them. "It was

164

good luck that we happened to be passing at the right moment." He looked at Sophie then continued, "This is Miss Sophie Allendale."

Herr Mittelmeyer took her hand and raised it to his lips, kissed it, then told her, "I am most happy to meet you and I hope you will visit us again." He turned to Robert. "You will bring her, yes?"

Robert, who was busy examining the patient, glanced up for a moment and answered, "I certainly will," then continued with his examination.

"There," he said as he straightened up, "your wife is improving. Her pulse is still too fast, but it is regular now. I advise that she should go to bed now and stay there for at least twenty-four hours. I think she should contact her own doctor tomorrow and tell him what has happened."

"I will see that she does," her husband assured them.

"Good! Then Sophie and I will be off. We're both on duty early tomorrow, but we'll meet again soon."

"I hope so, and bring the Fräulein with you any time she would like to visit us." Herr Mittelmeyer beamed. "I approve of your choice, Robert."

"Thank you," Sophie and Robert answered in unison.

"*Auf wiedersehen*, and take care of your wife."

"I will, you can be sure. *Auf wiedersehen*."

At the car Robert glanced at his watch then asked, "What do you say to a short run to get some fresh air into our lungs?"

"A marvellous idea." Sophie's response was immediate and full of enthusiasm. Anything that would prolong the time with him would meet with her approval.

They drove in an easterly direction for about ten kilometres then Robert turned off the *autobahn* on to a minor road where the ground rose steadily to the top of a hill. It was there that he drew into the side and turned off the engine.

For a few moments they sat in silence, admiring the beauty of the sky dappled with millions of star points. A commercial plane crossed the glittering mass, looking like a shooting star. Away in the distance they could see moonlight glistening on water, and beyond that the darkness of the *Teutoburger Wald*.

"This is my favourite look-out point," Robert spoke softly as though he did not want to disturb the peace and beauty of it all. "If I'm worried or restless I always escape to this. Somehow I can think more clearly when I'm here."

"I can understand that, it's so peaceful and lovely." Sophie, too, whispered, afraid of breaking the spell of the evening. "I wish we could stay here forever."

Robert turned to face her and, without warning, pulled her towards him. The kiss that followed was even more magical than the one he had given her at Christmas. She responded now with all the yearning and warmth of her nature.

"If only this heavenly feeling could last," she told herself but all thoughts were swamped in the elation she felt now then it was broken when Robert lifted his head and in a voice that held a note of despair murmured,

"Oh! Sophie, Sophie, I think I'm falling in love with you and I can't help myself. If only we had met a long time ago." Then before she could say anything her lips were covered again and the world and Robert's remark were forgotten.

When he at last released her all he said was, "We must be getting back." Then, without another word he started the engine and returned the way they had come.

Few words were spoken on the homeward journey, but Sophie was wrapped in a world of her own fantasy. It was not until they were near to the hospital that the second half of his astonishing statement hit her with its full significance.

Why was he reluctant to fall in love with her? And what was wrong with doing just that, she kept asking herself. The only answer she could find to the riddle was that he must be married already. She was still puzzled when he gave her a quick kiss outside her Mess and with a curt "good night", left her.

For the next week she saw little of him except on the ward during his daily round and, as the days passed, the invisible barrier was again firmly in place.

Because she was so deeply hurt by his attitude she knew she also had withdrawn into herself and that it was affecting her attitude towards him and everyone else. Once or twice he had been about to say something and she had turned away, or said the first thing that came into her mind about the patients. She had even on two occasions made an excuse and let Joyce do the ward round with Robert. It was only when she was with the patients that she relaxed at all. However unhappy she might be she was determined that they would not suffer through her.

One morning during coffee break Joyce asked her outright, "What's the matter between you and Robert? He hardly ever comes to see us now, and when he does he's restless and unhappy. Can Clive or I do anything to help?"

"No, no one can help," Sophie answered. "It's something I must work out for myself."

About a week later a patient who had been admitted the previous morning suddenly developed chest pains, a fever and difficulty in breathing. Sophie was on duty and phoned Robert to ask him to come and see her as soon as possible.

"'It looks like acute pneumonia," she told him.

The examination over, Robert turned to the patient and explained to her, "You have lobar pneumonia, but it's nothing to worry about. I'll give you an antibiotic right away, and within a day or two you'll be feeling much better." He entered the treatment he had ordered on her medical sheet before adding, "Sister will take care of you, so don't worry."

"Thank you, doctor."

Sophie glanced at him across the patient and saw something in his eyes that set her heart fluttering, but the look had been so transitory that she decided that it had been born of her own imagination.

When Sophie had given her orders to the SEN on duty what to give the patient, she returned to her office to find Robert waiting there for her. For once she appeared unsure of himself, uneasy she thought was a better word.

There was a faint hesitancy in his voice when he asked, "Will you have dinner with me tonight?"

At first Sophie was inclined to say no, not because she did not want to go but because she thought she would not be picked up and discarded whenever he chose to do so. Then her love won her over and she accepted, then regretted it.

When Robert had left her she sat thinking. Why did he act so strangely, so unpredictably? There was something to the whole situation that she could not fathom but what it was she had no idea. Her first thought had been that he might be married, but she had dismissed that idea long ago. He was much too honest and outspoken to be afraid to tell her if he had been.

Perhaps one day he might tell her but until that day

she decided to accept things as they were and be grateful for his companionship from time to time. Whatever his trouble was, it was something that went very deep, something about which he was either ashamed or just reluctant to reveal.

CHAPTER ELEVEN

So the bitter-sweet days continued then one morning, following a most pleasant evening spent with Robert with the promise of more to come, Doug came back into Sophie's life. She had just gone to her quarters to freshen up before returning to the ward when she was called to the telephone.

"It's a Dr. Courtenay," the telephonist told Sophie.

"Doug! What on earth is he ringing Germany for?" she asked herself. "What did he want?" It was with some apprehension that she waited for his voice to come over the line. Perhaps it was just coincidence, and it was another doctor of the same name.

"Sophie! How are you, darling?" She was no longer in doubt.

"I'm fine, thanks. Where are you ringing from?"

"Radlau. I crossed last night and arrived here less than an hour ago."

"But what are you doing in Germany?" Sophie knew the question was a foolish one.

"To see you, and I want to do that as soon as you can make it. What time are you off duty?"

"I'm on my way to the ward now, and will be there until five."

"I'll pick you up around five-thirty then." Sophie had little option but to accept, although she was reluctant to do so.

Doug had changed very little, but there was a faint air of humility about him that she had never known before. It was so strange she felt a sudden wave of affection for him and knew that however she might argue that he was nothing to her any more, some of her feelings were still bound up with him. It was an extraordinary feeling and one that Sophie did not particularly welcome. She was no longer in love with him, of that she was sure; so what was the attraction that had survived so much, despite her being in love with another man? It's a ridiculous situation, and I must be a ridiculous person, she decided as she got into the car.

"Let's drive out of town and find somewhere where we can talk," Doug suggested. "I've so much to say and to tell you, then we'll find a nice quiet place for dinner." He put his hand over hers for a moment then smiled at her. "You look lovelier than ever though you're more mature, very much a woman. There's something else, a serenity about you that I don't remember."

"Serenity? I certainly don't feel serene," she retorted.

"Neither do I, not when I'm with you," he added light-heartedly.

Sophie was about to explain that it wasn't because of him that she did not feel serene but because of another man, the man she really loved.

To change to a less personal theme she asked, "Where are you staying?"

"In the Mess, the RAMC of course. Giles Redmond, one of the new MOs, was at school with me and we've always kept in touch. Have you met him?"

"No, I'd heard there were two new doctors but I haven't seen either of them yet."

They had been driving in a westerly direction when Doug pointed to a road leading to what looked like a nature reserve.

"That looks as good a place as any," he remarked, and she agreed. Whatever he wanted to say to her, the sooner it was said the better it would be for her peace of mind. Parking near the entrance, Doug guided her through the gates and towards a vacant seat only a few yards inside.

When they were seated Sophie waited for him to speak. She was determined not to make it easy for him; he was the one who had been the cause of the trouble between them, she had only made the final break.

Doug began to speak slowly and Sophie was convinced that he was weighing up every word before uttering it. He also paused for effect every now and then and as he talked all the humility had disappeared and his supreme self-confidence was back.

"Darling, I love you and want you to give me a second chance and say that you'll marry me. You loved me once, so you can't have changed all that much. You're not the changing type, you're a one-man girl."

Sophie hesitated before she spoke in a cold, deliberate voice. "I may be as you say, but I don't love you any more. You killed that, remember? It wasn't from choice that I broke off our engagement."

"I accept all the blame, but it was over nothing really. I told you at the time that it was you whom I loved. I've said how sorry I am for my lapse and that's all it was." He looked thoroughly aggrieved. "What more can I say?"

"Nothing, but Doug, I mean it when I say it's all over between us. There's nothing left, not now."

"What do you mean, not now? Is there another man?"

Her hesitation was only fractional, but she saw the doubt registered on Doug's face, and before she could answer he continued aggressively, "There *is* another man. Who is he? Are you going to marry him?"

"I've no plans to marry anyone at the moment. I

have been asked by one man, but as I didn't love him I turned him down. Does that answer your question?"

"Yes, but there's the other question, will you marry me?"

"I'm sorry, Doug, but the answer is no," Sophie said patiently. "I couldn't go through all that misery and doubt again with any man, not even you."

"But I've changed," he protested. "Like you I've matured, learned common sense."

"I really am sorry but the answer is still no."

"Well I'm here for a week, during which time I intend keeping up the pressure until you do change your mind." Sophie did not miss the look of cunning that momentarily appeared in his eyes as he finished speaking.

She felt a deep sense of misgiving overcome her when she remembered how devious he could be to get his own way. She felt afraid for the future; not of physical violence but because Doug always had been able to scheme his way in and out of any situation. She had been blind to his faults in those early days, but now she saw them with a clarity that was alarming.

Changing his tactics, he asked, "You will at least see me while I'm here, won't you, for the sake of what we once had?"

"Very well," she answered, but she knew she was being foolish. However she too had changed, and she was much more sophisticated and more capable of holding her own, even against Doug's charm, which she knew could be quite formidable. Her thoughts were interrupted by him asking,

"Let's go find a place for dinner. Some place of your choosing, as I don't know Germany very well." Suddenly he braked. "There's a likely looking place, what about that?"

"No!" Sophie had not meant to be so emphatic but it was the restaurant where Robert had taken her once or twice. She felt she could not bear to go there with Doug. In a quieter voice she added, "There's one about three kilometres back where I've been once. It's small but the food is good." It was a place that she was sure she would not run into anyone from the hospital, especially Robert.

It turned out to be quite a pleasant evening as Doug did not attempt to force his attentions on her except by turning on the charm. Most of their conversation was about St Andrew's and their many mutual friends. When he took her home his goodnight kiss was not demanding but gentle and short, for which she was most grateful.

She became lulled into a feeling of false security after three such evenings then came the night she told him she could not meet him the following evening, Saturday. "I already have a date which I can't break," she told him.

"Who's the date with, Robert or Martin?"

"Robert," she answered, surprised that he should know exactly who her special friends were. "But what's that to you? My friends are entirely my own concern, surely?"

"Not entirely, for two good reasons; one, that I have some claim on you because of our engagement which you broke, and my own determination to marry you. The second is that I've come all this way to see you, and will only be here for another three days, so I think you owe me that much."

"I owe you nothing, nothing at all," she replied, amazed at his arrogance.

Doug faced her with a look of intense anger and with

lips compressed into a thin line, then he forced a smile as he informed her, "But you still love me, even if you do try to deny it."

"Of all the egotistical, conceited individuals you take first prize! I once loved you but I certainly do not love you now." She got no further because Doug's mouth was on hers in a kiss both demanding and hurtful.

For a brief moment Sophie felt herself responding then she tried to pull away. She felt humiliated that she should have shown any degree of response to this man she no longer loved. The thought of her love for Robert only succeeded in making her more confused and angry. When she finally managed to free herself Doug smiled, obviously pleased with himself.

"Now tell me you don't love me." There was exultation in his voice and a look of amusement in his eyes.

Momentarily Sophie could not speak as she tried to compose herself. Her dominating thought was to get away from this man, away from the shame of feeling like this for one man when she was in love with another.

When she spoke her voice was decidedly chilly. "No, I don't love you, and I can't see you tomorrow night. You'll be leaving on Tuesday, so I'll keep Sunday and Monday evening free if you'd like me to for the sake of our friendship, nothing more."

"Very well," he agreed. "If that's your decision I suppose I must accept it. However I can still hope."

He leant forward to kiss her but she evaded him and jumping from the car called, "Goodnight," and was soon in bed but not to sleep for some time. It was early morning when she wakened feeling confused and unhappy. All she longed for was Doug's departure on Tuesday. Then she remembered her date with Robert and her mood lightened.

When Robert had finished his round that morning the last thing he said to her was, "I'll call for you at seven. I'm taking you somewhere quiet as I want to talk to you, and to tell you something I should have told you a long time ago." Then he had looked directly at her and smiled. In addition to the smile there was a look in his eyes that set Sophie's heart fluttering and made her long for the evening to come.

Now as he ran down the stairs she felt happiness had added wings to her feet.

"You're looking full of the joys tonight, Sophie," one of her friends called as she passed.

"I am," she replied as she hurried on towards the anteroom where Robert always met her, but the man who rose to greet her was not Robert.

"What are you doing here, Doug? I told you that I wasn't free tonight," she asked sharply.

"Your friend Robert can't make it so I'm deputising for him."

"But why can't he make it, and why did he send you instead of contacting me himself?" she demanded in deep dismay.

"Your phone was engaged so I offered to bring you the message and to take you out to enjoy yourself." There was a smile of satisfaction on his face as he continued, "I've booked a table for us at the Hungaria for seven-thirty. I'm told it's a first-class place where you can dance and see a cabaret as well. I'm going to show you something of German life at its best."

Sophie was about to turn down his invitation because of the deep hurt she felt at Robert's casualness and to cancel at the very last minute like that. Why? she kept repeating to herself. And after telling her that he especially wanted to talk to her! She was not only hurt but puzzled. It was so unlike Robert to be rude. The thought of ringing him passed through her mind, but her pride would not allow her to do that. Anyway, why should she stay at home and be miserable when she could go out and enjoy an evening with an old friend?

"All right, Doug, let's go," she told him with forced gaiety.

When she saw the look of gratification on his face she had a moment of indecision. Had he told her everything? Surely even he would not sink so low as to misrepresent the situation. Anyway it was done now. She had accepted his invitation, so she might as well relax and enjoy the evening.

The Hungaria was a pleasant restaurant, though a little on the noisy side. It was was much larger than any Sophie had been to, and more crowded. Looking quickly around she could see no familiar faces and she judged that most of the guests were German.

It was obvious from the start that Doug was out to charm her if he could. In the past she had always fallen for it, but now she could clearly see through it. Still full of hurt pride and bitterness at Robert's casual cancellation of their date, Sophie decided that she would enjoy herself and it was in that mood that she responded to his advances. By the time they finished their main course she felt more relaxed.

"Let's dance," Doug suggested. "We can order the sweet when we get back to the table."

The small band was first class with a good sense of rhythm and, though they could only shuffle in a very confined area, Sophie found herself actually enjoying it. Doug was a superb dancer and she had always found him very easy to follow. Now some of the old glamour of their association in London returned.

"Enjoying yourself?" he asked when they were dancing.

"Mmm. You know I've always loved dancing."

There were two acts during the cabaret. One a German singer with a backing trio whose harmony was better than the singer himself. The other act was a magician. It was a clever performance and one that Sophie enjoyed very much. Even the thought of Robert could not dispel the feeling of pleasure she derived from his perfection. It was only on the drive home that the hurt returned in full force to spoil the evening.

As Doug was leaving Radlau on Tuesday, Sophie had arranged to have all day Monday off and a morning pass for Tuesday. She felt she owed him that much of her time. As he had said, he had come a long way to see her.

Although she found those days enjoyable Robert was never far from her mind. She still found his behaviour strange and completely out of character. Unless there was an emergency on Tuesday afternoon on the ward she would not see him until Wednesday when he came to do his round. Obviously he was not going to make an opportunity to see her and explain. She felt deeply resentful, and was determined that he would have to make the first overture. She would be cold and withdrawn just as he could be.

On Monday Sophie suggested to Doug that they go and see the Möhne Dam. "It's quite a long way, but you shouldn't leave Germany without seeing it."

"Okay, and Sophie, thank you for getting time off especially for me."

She almost blurted out, "Don't be so complacent. I'm only doing it for an old friend, nothing more," but managed to restrain herself and substituted, "As it was your last day I felt it was the least I could do."

Whether it was the result of his complacency, and his assumption that he had her where he wanted her, that had any bearing on the day she was not sure, but somehow things seemed to go wrong from the moment the car drew away from the Mess. It was only by asserting a good deal of self control that Sophie stopped from snapping at her companion on several occasions. On Doug's part he was more conceited than she had ever known him to be. To add to her discomfiture it began to rain just as they were walking across the dam to see the Dambusters' bomb.

"We may as well keep going now," she told him as she tied a scarf over her hair. "There! Have you ever seen anything like that?" There was excitement and wonder in her voice as she pointed to the large metal object.

"Well, it's what one would expect," rejoined Doug. "I knew it would need to be an unconventional shape, otherwise they would never have been able to bounce it as they did."

"You may have, but I certainly didn't. I think it looks more like a space ship than a bomb."

"But then you're a woman, and not expected to know about these things." His reply only made things worse.

"Don't be so ... condescending," she shot back at him and flounced back towards the bridge.

"Darling, don't be in such a hurry. I didn't mean to upset you."

"I'm getting wet," was all she said as she hurried on her way.

"Come on, love. Don't let's quarrel now. I'm off tomorrow. Let's go and have lunch, and then we can drive wherever you may choose and have a quiet supper along the way or go into Münster and have it there. We can decide later."

The rest of the day passed pleasantly enough, but Sophie was not at all sorry when the car stopped outside the QA Mess. She turned to Doug and caught a strange look on his face. What was it; satisfaction, smugness, or was it something quite different?

It certainly wasn't sadness or regret at saying good-bye which might have been expected, if he loved her as he said he did.

Well, whatever it was it was not worth worrying about, but she would like to get this goodbye over.

"Doug, it has been nice seeing you and if you ever return to Germany get in touch," she told him from mere politeness.

"Get in touch! Too damned right I will." The look of incredulity on his face made her want to laugh, but she managed to restrain herself as he continued, "I'm hoping to take you away from it for ever."

"Please, Doug. When I told you it was all over between us I meant it."

"Is it?" and with that he pulled her roughly towards him and kissed her hard and long. Once more Sophie felt that physical response, but this time managed to pull away. However her rejection of him could not have registered, because in a voice filled with triumph he added, "Now say it's all over between us," and once more put his arms around her.

Suddenly a feeling of revulsion surged through her, and pulling away roughly from his arms, she turned on him, anger in her voice, her eyes blazing. "Yes, it *is* over, irrevocably, and I never want to see you again," and meant what she said because at last she realised that every atom of feeling for him had gone. She was completely free, all doubt swept away.

Something in her expression must have registered at last with Doug, for he made no further attempt to detain her. All he said was, "All right, but if you should ever change your mind, just get in touch. I'm hoping to get a Consultancy before long and from there I hope to move into Harley Street, so if I'm not at Andrew's you'll know where you can contact me."

"Yes, I'll know, but I doubt that I shall ever change my mind," Sophie said more calmly. "Anyway, all the luck in the world, and I hope you'll find a wife who will suit you. I'm not cut out for the Harley Street scene, so you should think yourself lucky that you've escaped."

Doug shrugged, "Perhaps you're right. Goodbye, Sophie, and whatever you say I still wish I could have made you change your mind."

Sophie turned at the top of the steps and waved to him as he moved off. She felt no sadness at his going. As she entered the Mess she decided to glance in the pigeonhole in case there was any mail for her. There was a letter from her parents and a scrawled note from Clare which read,

"Robert phoned twice. He left no message. Hope you've had a whale of a time, love, Clare."

Some whale of a time, Sophie thought despondently but her spirit lightened when she thought that Robert had tried to contact her. He may have been too busy to do so earlier, she argued to herself. If it wasn't quite so late she would have phoned him then, but it was after eleven.

On Tuesday afternoon Sophie went on duty with mixed feelings. Everyone on the ward seemed pleased to see her. Joyce greeted her with, "Nice to see you back. Hope you had a lovely time."

It was not until after Matron's round the following morning that Joyce had an opportunity to ask, "What's gone wrong between you and Robert? He spent the evening with us on Saturday and we could hardly get a word out of him, and I've never seen him so moody. One minute he seemed quite angry and the next full of self-pity. When I asked him what was wrong he just murmured something about being let down, but he wouldn't explain further."

"Did he mention that I let him down?" asked Sophie.

"No, he gave no names, but I hope it has nothing to do with you. You're the first girl he's ever taken seriously ever since I've known him. I'm very fond of him and hate to see him looking so low. You were supposed to be going out with him on Saturday, weren't you?"

"Yes, but he sent a message by Doug to tell me he couldn't make it. There were no explanations of any kind. I asked Doug specially." Sophie was momentarily silent then added, "But I don't want to talk about Robert."

"Okay, love. I'm sorry if I'm being too nosy."

Sophie responded to the hurt look in her friend's eyes. "It's nothing like that. I only wish I did know what went wrong. I can't think of anything I've done to cause any upset, but I'm as puzzled as you are." Further talk was interrupted by Robert himself.

In a very cold manner he asked Sophie, "Ready to do a ward round now, Sister?"

"Yes, sir." Her own tone was even more frigid than his.

However chaotic the doctor's and sister's feelings might be, neither of them showed it in front of their patients. Robert was his usual bland self just as Sophie remained the calm, kindly, trained nursing officer. It was only when the round finished and they were on their way to the duty office that she hoped he might forward some explanation for his action in cancelling their date. Just as he stood aside to allow her to pass in front of her his bleep started. With a hurried apology he lifted the phone and Sophie heard him say, "Right. I'll be over immediately." He turned to her with a muttered "Sorry" and dashed off before she had a chance to say anything.

For the next two days Robert was away at one of the outer stations doing clinics. On the ward everything passed without incident. The junior doctor, Captain Bellamy, who took over Robert's rounds in his absence, was a nice young man but was lacking in Robert's experience. However, as there were no crises the routine of the ward continued on its usual smooth and efficient way under Sophie's complete dedication.

But, despite her absorption with her work, there was a bleakness about her life such as she had never experienced before. Thank goodness there was the chance of her going to surgical in a week or two! She never thought she would welcome that change but now she was looking forward to it. One thing she would find out before she moved was why Robert had cancelled their date. She felt she deserved to know that much.

On the following Monday Robert had finished his round and had gone down to the laboratory to see some results for himself. Sophie, once more regretful that she had not forced an explanation from him, was sitting alone in her office and feeling decidedly dejected. She did not hear Robert return or realise that he was standing in the doorway gazing at her back. There was an air of desolation about her that smote him forcibly. Doubts formed in his mind that he might possibly have misjudged her.

Could she be loyal and honest as he had thought her to be before Doug came back into her life? Or was she like Christine, all love and sweetness on the outside but secretly always ready to sell herself to the highest bidder? Somehow that impression no longer convinced him. She should at least be given the opportunity to clear herself and not just be condemned out of hand. After all, he only had Doug's word to go on. Making up his mind he asked,

"When are you getting married?"

Sophie stared at him in consternation. "Who said I was getting married?"

"Your fiancé, of course. Douglas Courtenay, remember him?" His voice was cold though he had not meant it to be.

"He isn't my fiancé," she replied vehemently. "He was a long time ago, before I came to Germany. I broke it off then."

"But you spent all your time with him when he was here and preferred to go out with him on the Saturday when you had already arranged to go with me. I tried to phone you on several occasions, but you were always out."

"I did spend a good deal of time with him, but I repeat, I'm not engaged to him nor am I likely to be, and he knows that as well as I do," she said firmly. "As to your allegation that *I* broke our date it's completely untrue. *You* broke it."

"Look, Sophie, we can't talk here. Will you dine with me tonight? I know just the place." Suddenly he grinned and his cold aloofness was transformed immediately into something warm and promising.

Sophie paused in an effort to calm the wild beating of her heart before accepting his invitation. "But I'm on duty until eight," she added.

"Then I'll call for you at half-past, and will wait until you're ready."

"I'll be ready."

Sophie had never hurried as she did to bath and change that evening. She chose a dark blue patterned dress that Robert had not seen before. She was just

184

applying the last touch of make-up when someone called to her that Doctor Austin was waiting for her in the anteroom.

The look he gave her when she joined him was full of admiration but she kept a tight rein on her own feelings, though she was not aware that the expression in her eyes revealed her secret. As they walked towards the car Robert took her hand, something he had never done before. Happiness surged through her at his touch.

"The restaurant I'm taking you to is owned by a friend of mine. He is German and a very nice man. His father was killed by our troops in the last war, but he bears us no grudge. I'm sure you'll like him, and we can talk there for as long as we wish."

The words *What are we going to talk about?* trembled on her lips but she held them back. She could wait a little longer.

When at last they were seated at the table, Sophie's heart was no longer beating wildly, it was creating a positive tattoo within her, but she hoped Robert could not hear it.

When the meal was ordered and they had both had an aperitif, Robert told her, "First of all I'd like to apologise for not insisting on contacting you direct on that Saturday your fiancé – ex-fiancé," he interrupted her intended denial, "was here. He gave me to understand not only that you were engaged, but that you wanted to go out with him but did not want to disappoint me at the last moment. What really hurt was that you had kept your engagement a secret and had not shown enough courage to cancel our date yourself."

When Sophie was about to interject he held up his hand. "No, let me carry on. You can say whatever you like when I've finished. Until that time I had really thought we had something going for us and that, at last, I had found a girl who could be true and loyal. When I learned what I believed to be the truth I was devastated. I was determined then, for the second time, never to become involved emotionally with a girl again."

"What do you mean again?"

"I was engaged to a girl I loved very much but she threw me over when a better proposition came along. I thought I would never get over it but I did and when I met you Christine became a dim memory."

"Christine, isn't that your stepmother?"

He nodded," Yes, Christine ditched me for my father. He was an established Harley Street consultant, I was nothing but a junior registrar earning less than some of the untrained staff."

Sophie gasped, "Oh! Robert, I'm so sorry. No wonder you were so cold and unbending, and I can understand why you thought I had let you down. You should have known me better than that."

"I thought I did, but I suppose my stupid pride wouldn't let me ask."

"Surely you could have telephoned me instead of sending a message through Doug?"

"I tried on several occasions, but you know what telephones are like. There's always someone chatting on them. When I eventually got through you had already gone out. I did leave a message with someone, didn't you get that?"

"No. If I had I would have spoken about the evening when you were on the ward. When you never mentioned it I decided that you would have to make the first move."

Robert gave a half smile. "Doug seems to have played us one against the other very cleverly, doesn't he?"

"He most certainly did! He always has been devious

but I'd never have thought he would have gone to such lengths."

"Let's forget about him. He can't hurt us any more." Robert stretched out his hand and took hers. As she gazed at him across the table she saw love and happiness shining in his blue eyes and suddenly all the doubts, the conflict and the misunderstandings were gone as though they had never existed. Sophie felt herself aglow with happiness as he began to speak again.

"Let's get out of here as soon as I've settled my bill. We have a lot to talk about."

In the car Robert did not kiss her as she had expected but drove straight to a *parkplatz* a couple of kilometres from the restaurant. There he turned to her and opened his mouth to speak, but what he saw in her face made him forget all the things he had planned to say. Instead he drew her into his arms and kissed her long and lovingly. Sophie found herself drifting into a state of complete euphoria as she responded to his tenderness and the promise of a happiness she had never imagined could be hers.

When he lifted his head he whispered, "I've been such a blind, blind fool. Oh, Sophie, I love you, will you marry me?"

She heard the love and longing in his voice and answered without hesitation, "I will."

He kissed her gently and she knew that here was a man revealed in his true qualities, a man she could love and trust with all the depth of which she was capable. The façade he had worn for so long had disappeared and in its place sat a man beloved and loving. When he started to explain why he had always appeared so withdrawn from her she put her fingers to his lips.

"No, darling," she told him quietly. "I realise I was

as much to blame, so let's wipe the slate clean and start to build a new world for ourselves."

"We'll certainly do that, but there's one promise I must ask of you; if there are ever any doubts in your mind about us it must be brought out into the open. Will you make a pact on that now? I promise to keep it whatever my stupid pride may dictate. Will you?"

"I promise. There is no other way to complete happiness without honesty in all things between us." Then Sophie held up her face for his kiss to seal the pact.

Overhead the stars shone brighter and the moon, partially covered by a small isolated cloud, emerged in full beauty to smile down on them. At the same moment a night bird in a nearby tree began to sing quietly but beautifully as though rejoicing with the lovers in their happiness.

Simultaneously Sophie and Robert looked up to see if they could locate it just as a jet looking like a shooting star shot across their vision.

In a hushed voice Sophie said, "Everything looks so beautiful tonight doesn't it?"

"Everything, but nothing so beautiful as you, Sophie, my love." Then his lips covered hers once more.

Further words were unnecessary, this kiss said it all for them. This was a love that had been worth waiting and suffering for. Whatever the future might hold for them they knew that together they could face anything. The past was forgotten; only the future stretched ahead of them, its path shining and bright.

Also available this month
Four Titles in our Mills & Boon
Classics Series

*Specially chosen re-issues of the best in
Romantic Fiction*

May's Titles are:

DARE I BE HAPPY?
by Mary Burchell

Marigold should have been blissfully happy in her marriage
to Paul Irving — but how could she, when the one man in the
world who could wreck it with a word was Paul's own
brother-in-law?

THE CASTLE OF THE SEVEN LILACS
by Violet Winspear

When the handsome Baron Breck von Linden offered Siran
a job which involved staying at his fairytale home, the
Castle of the Seven Lilacs, she knew that it was attraction
for the Baron that was taking her there. But Breck's younger
brother Kurt made no secret of his opinion of Siran and
her motives. . . . .

A MAN WITHOUT MERCY
by Margery Hilton

Compassion and loyalty — two endearing qualities, but they
had brought Gerda nothing but heartbreak. Compassion had
led her into a brief, tragic marriage. Now loyalty had forced
her into the power of the one man who could destroy her.
Because she loved Jordan Black as much as he despised her
— and he was a man without mercy . . . . .

SOUTH TO FORGET
by Essie Summers

After an unhappy love affair Mary Rose wanted to get away
from everything, so when Ninian Macandrew, who had also
recently been jilted, asked her to go to his New Zealand
home with him as his fiancée it seemed the solution to her
problems. But "Oh what a tangled web we weave, when
first we practise to deceive"!

Mills & Boon Classics
— all that's great in Romantic Reading!
BUY THEM TODAY only 50p